Where Leo Died

A Legal Suspense Thriller

Howard Kane

Hidden Alpha Capital LLC

About the author

Howard Kane writes the stories most people are afraid to tell.

As a former Fortune 500 executive, he knows what it feels like to appear successful on the outside while quietly unraveling on the inside. For years, he hid his drinking behind late nights, busy calendars, and a polished smile. When he finally faced the truth about his addiction, he discovered that recovery wasn't just possible; it was life-changing.

Howard channels that experience into memoir-style novels that explore addiction, family trauma, money, and power. His five-book saga, The Daughter of a Drunk, follows Olivia Parker from a terrified little girl in a small Ohio town, vowing she'll never be like her father, to a woman fighting billionaires, corrupt institutions, and her own worst impulses. The series blends coming-of-age drama, generational alcoholism, and high-stakes whistleblower suspense into one continuous, bingeable story.

He also writes standalone novels rooted in alcohol dependence and recovery, including The Double Life of a High-Functioning Alcoholic, which pulls back the curtain on the addiction that hides behind ambition and success, and From Wine Mom to Sober Mom, which shines a light on the unique struggles mothers face when drinking threatens everything they love.

Through raw honesty and lived experience, Howard's books show that surviving a drunk parent or being the drunk parent is only the beginning. The real story is what you do with the wreckage. Readers describe his work as "impossible to put down" because the characters feel uncomfortably real, and their choices never come cheap.

If you've ever questioned your relationship with drinking, grown up in the shadow of someone else's, or wondered how far you'd go to protect the people you love, Howard Kane's stories are for you.

Website: https://selfcarejourneybooks.com/

Contents

Chapter One

Everything Breaking

THE PHONE RANG AT 6:47 AM on a Tuesday. Richard's name appeared on the screen. My banker. The man who helped me invest the settlement money. The man who warned me not to do this. I knew before I answered. Like sensing an impending car accident. Like knowing someone is about to die. That certainty in my bones that everything's about to break.

Grace was almost three, sitting at the kitchen table, sorting her cereal by color. Again and again. The same motion. Over and over. Her brain fixated on patterns because FASD made everything harder. Simple tasks became compulsions. Red pieces in one pile. Yellow in another. Blue. Green. Starting over when they mixed.

"Mama, look." She held up a red piece. "Red."

"Good job, baby."

She returned to sorting. I picked up the phone.

"Hello?"

"Olivia." Richard's voice was tight. Professional but scared. "We need to talk. Now."

My stomach dropped. A physical sensation of falling.

"The margin call?"

"Yes. CMG dropped to $6.50 this morning. Down another 13% overnight. You're now at 72% of required maintenance."

The numbers didn't make sense at first. Like hearing a forgotten language. Then they did. I'd bought CMG at $10 per share. My analysis indicated it was worth $60-70. Undervalued by more than 80%. A bargain. The opportunity of a lifetime. But the market didn't care about my analysis. It was panicking. Selling everything. Driving prices lower and lower. $10 to $8 to $7.50 to $6.50. A 35% drop from my purchase price.

"How much?" My voice came out strangled.

"You need to deposit $480,000 by Friday at 4 PM. If you can't, we liquidate your entire position automatically. No discussion. No extension. That's the agreement you signed."

$480,000. Seventy-two hours.

Grace dropped her spoon. The clatter was too loud. Metal on tile. My whole body flinched.

"Olivia? Do you understand what I'm telling you?"

I understood. I'd borrowed $5 million against my $5.5 million to buy stock. Used margin to amplify my bet. Bought 10.2% of Carrington Media Group at $10 per share. The stock was now at $6.50. Down 35%.

"My analysis was right." The words came out desperate. "The company's worth $60-70 per share. The fundamentals are solid. Core business generates $80 million in cash flow. It's just—"

"It's just the market doesn't care about your analysis right now." Richard's voice was gentle but firm. "Panic selling. Fear. That's what drives prices in the short term. And short term, you're about to lose everything."

"But I'm right! The valuation—"

"Olivia." He cut me off. "Being right doesn't matter if you run out of money before the market realizes it. That's what margin does. It amplifies gains, but it also amplifies losses. And it has a deadline."

He paused. I heard papers rustling.

"Look, I probably shouldn't tell you this, but there's been unusual activity in CMG lately. Big volume. Someone's been accumulating shares. A shark is sniffing around. But whoever it is hasn't made any public announcement yet, and they might never. You can't count on that."

A shark. Someone big buying. But Richard was right. It didn't matter unless they announced it. Unless they moved the market. And I had seventy-two hours.

Grace was looking at me, her face filled with concern, like toddlers do when they sense something's wrong even if they can't understand it. "Mama sad?"

I couldn't answer. Couldn't breathe. Couldn't think.

"You have 72 hours," Richard said. "After that, we sell. You'll walk away with almost nothing from your original $5.5 million. Everything else goes to covering the loan. Do you understand?"

I understood. I could lose everything. Grace's future. Her medical fund. Her education. Everything I'd built. Gone. Because I'd used borrowed money to bet on a collapsing company.

"Yes," I whispered. "I understand."

"I'm sorry, Olivia. I really am. I warned you this could happen. But I'd hoped—" His voice broke. "I'd hoped I was wrong."

He hung up. I stood there holding the phone, the kitchen tilting. Grace was looking at me with those eyes. Leo's eyes. Concerned, scared, and knowing something was very wrong.

"Mama sad?"

I ran to the bathroom and made it to the toilet just before I vomited.

Linda found me on the bathroom floor twenty minutes later. Grace was screaming. Not crying. Screaming. The high-pitched sound she made when Mama was gone too long. When her world felt unsafe.

"Olivia?" Linda's voice was sharp and scared. "What happened? Grace is—"

She stopped, saw my face, saw me on the cold tile, shaking.

"Oh God. What happened?"

I couldn't speak. Couldn't form words. Just shook my head. Linda knelt down and put her hand on my back. Warm. Solid. Real.

"Breathe. Just breathe. Tell me what happened."

"Margin call." The words tasted like ash, like vodka I hadn't drunk in years. "I have 72 hours to deposit $480,000 or they liquidate everything."

Linda's face went white. "Everything? The whole position?"

"Everything."

Grace's screaming grew louder and more desperate. Linda stood up fast.

"I'll get her. You... just stay here. Just breathe."

She left. I heard her voice soothing Grace, heard Grace's sobs, heard Linda carrying her away. Bath water running. The routine that sometimes helped reset Grace's nervous system when the world got too big.

I sat on the bathroom floor, cold tile against my legs. Dad used to pass out on this floor. Alone. Surrounded by empty bottles. I was sober. Four years sober. But I was still on a bathroom floor at 7 AM. Still destroying everything. Still becoming him. Just a different poison. Not vodka. Revenge.

I eventually made it to the kitchen. I don't know how long I sat there at first. Linda had Grace in the bath. I could hear splashing and Linda's voice, soft and steady. Grace was quieter now. The water was helping.

My laptop was on the table. I opened it and stared at my brokerage account. I'd invested $10.5 million: $5.5 million of my own, $5 million borrowed. Now it was worth $6.8 million, and I owed $5 million. Net equity: $1.8 million.

From $5.5 million to $1.8 million in less than eight weeks. I'd lost $3.7 million. More than two-thirds. And it was still dropping.

Eight weeks ago, when I bought at $10, the market cap had been $100 million. I thought that was the bottom. I was wrong. Panic still had room to run. The stock could hit $5, $4, or even zero if fear kept driving it down. I'd be liquidated long before it recovered.

Linda came in with Grace wrapped in a towel, her hair wet and her face calm now. The bath had helped.

"Grace wants you."

Grace reached for me. "Mama." I took her and held her against my chest. She was warm from the bath. Soft. Real. The most important thing in my life. And I'd just gambled her future on a stock trade.

"What are you going to do?" Linda asked quietly.

"I don't know." The words came out broken. "I don't have $480,000. I can't get it, can't borrow it, can't magic it into existence."

"So they'll sell?"

"Friday at 4 PM. Automatic. No discussion."

Linda sat down hard, Grace between us, looking at both of us with concerned eyes.

"How much will you have left?"

"Maybe something if the stock doesn't drop more before Friday. Maybe nothing. Depends on how far it falls."

Linda's face. I couldn't bear to look at it. Couldn't see the disappointment. The confirmation that I was exactly what she'd feared.

"You had $5.5 million," she said slowly. "You've already lost almost $3.7 million in eight weeks."

"Yes."

"Because you had to destroy Tyler. Because revenge was more important than Grace's future."

The words hit like fists.

"Mom—"

"No." She stood up and took Grace from my arms. "I need to think. You need to figure out what you'll tell your daughter when she asks why you gambled away her future."

She left, taking Grace upstairs. I sat alone at the kitchen table, staring at the numbers that had destroyed my life.

For the first two days after Richard's call, I could do nothing but watch the stock price fall. On Wednesday, it dropped to $5.80. On Thursday, it hit $5.10. I sat at the kitchen table, laptop open, watching the numbers destroy everything. Grace needed me, called for me, but I couldn't move or respond. Linda took over, made meals, played with Grace, put her to bed, and told her Mama was sick. She wasn't wrong.

By Thursday night, I'd lost nearly $5 million. Almost everything. Grace's future, her medical fund, her education. Gone. Because I'd borrowed money to bet on revenge.

I didn't sleep Thursday night. I lay in bed staring at the ceiling, listening to Grace breathe through the monitor and my own heartbeat. Too fast. Too loud.

At 3 AM, I got up and went to Grace's room. She was sleeping, thumb in her mouth, her face peaceful. She didn't know her mother had destroyed everything or that she'd have nothing. She didn't know I was the worst thing that ever happened to her.

I whispered in the darkness, "I'm sorry. I thought I could give you power, security, something Tyler couldn't take away."

My voice broke. "But I gave you nothing. I am nothing. Just my father's daughter after all." She stirred, made a small sound, then settled back into sleep.

I went to my room and opened the nightstand drawer. Dad's broken compass sat there, spinning for years. I picked it up. The needle spun now, frantic and lost. No north. No direction. Just chaos. Like me.

I thought about the vodka. Four years sober. Four years of fighting. For what? To end up here? To lose everything anyway? What was the point of staying sober if I destroyed Grace's life?

I put the compass back, closed the drawer, and sat on my bed in the dark. Thinking about vodka. About surrender. About the relief of stopping. But I didn't move. Didn't buy the vodka. Because even now, even at the bottom, a small part of me wouldn't let me become him completely. Some part still fought, even though it felt pointless.

The market opened at 9:30 AM on Friday. I was already at the table, laptop open, watching. The stock opened at $5.05, down another five cents overnight. Seven and a half hours until liquidation.

Linda came downstairs with Grace. She didn't speak to me, made breakfast for Grace, and put on cartoons. Grace ate her cereal, sorting it by color again. The same compulsion. Red. Yellow. Blue. Green. Over and over.

I watched the stock barely move, just sitting there around $5.10. No volume. No movement. Just dying. By 3 PM: $5.20. Up slightly from the morning. Going nowhere. I had one hour until liquidation. One hour until everything ended.

Grace wanted a snack. Linda made her cheese and crackers. Grace climbed into her chair, ate happily, humming to herself. She didn't know. Didn't understand. That in one hour, her future was gone.

3:30 PM. The stock was at $5.18. Thirty minutes left.

I should call Richard. Should tell him something. Should say goodbye to the money. Accept what was coming. But I couldn't move. Couldn't think. Just sat there, watching the clock, watching the stock, waiting for the end.

3:45 PM. Fifteen minutes. The stock ticked up to $5.22. Meaningless. Too late. I was still far below the maintenance requirement. A few cents didn't matter.

3:50 PM. Ten minutes. Grace came into the kitchen. "Mama, look!" She had a drawing of two stick figures under a sun.

"Who's that?" I made my voice work.

"You and me!" She smiled, proud.

"It's beautiful, baby."

She climbed onto my lap. Warm. Solid. Real. I held her and memorized how she felt. Because in ten minutes, I'd have to tell her that Mama lost everything. That Mama gambled her future and lost.

3:55 PM. Five minutes. The phone rang. Richard.

My hand shook as I reached for it.

"Hello?"

"Olivia." His voice was different. Confused. "Something just happened."

My heart stopped. "What?"

"A 13D filing just hit. Someone disclosed a 10% position in CMG. Activist investor. Big name."

I couldn't breathe. Couldn't process.

"Who?"

"David Keller. Titan Capital. He just announced he owns 10% and he's calling the company severely undervalued."

The room tilted.

"What does that mean?"

"It means..." Richard paused. "After-hours trading is about to get very interesting. Hold on."

I heard him typing. Heard him breathing.

"Olivia. The stock is moving. After-hours. It just jumped to $6.20."

$6.20. Up from $5.20.

"Does that cancel the margin call?"

"Not yet. But if it keeps going... if Keller's announcement creates momentum..."

His voice trailed off. I sat there, Grace in my lap, phone to my ear, not understanding. Not believing.

"I'll call you back," Richard said. "Watch the after-hours. This could change everything."

He hung up. I opened my laptop with shaking hands. Bloomberg alert. Posted at 4:02 PM.

BREAKING: ACTIVIST INVESTOR TITAN CAPITAL ANNOUNCES 10% STAKE IN CARRINGTON MEDIA

Titan Capital, led by legendary activist David Keller, announced late Friday it has acquired 10% of Carrington Media Group's outstanding shares. In a statement, Keller called the company "severely undervalued" and said Titan would push for "significant strategic and leadership changes." The announcement came after markets closed, with CMG trading at $5.20 per share.

After-hours trading ticker. $6.20 to $6.75 to $7.10. Moving up. Fast.

David Keller. Legendary activist. The man who destroyed CEOs for a living. Worth $4.2 billion. He'd bought 10% of CMG today, hours before my liquidation, and he'd told the world it was undervalued.

The market was listening. $7.10 to $7.35 to $7.50.

Grace was still in my lap, playing with my hair and humming. I couldn't move. Couldn't process what I was seeing.

"Mama?" Grace looked up at me. "You okay?"

"Yeah, baby. Mama's okay."

But I wasn't okay. I was watching something impossible. By 7 PM: $7.52. I refreshed my brokerage account. The numbers had changed.

Current Price: $7.52 (after-hours), Current Value: $7,671,000, Margin Call: REQUIRES ADDITIONAL RE-VIEW

Requires additional review. Not canceled. Not approved. Just pending. I wasn't at $5.20 anymore. Wasn't losing everything tomorrow. I was at $7.52. Down 24.8% from my purchase price. Still losing. Still hurting. But alive.

My phone rang. Richard again.

"Olivia. I've been reviewing your position."

"And?"

"The after-hours move brought you close to the maintenance requirement. Not quite there, but close enough for me to give you a 72-hour extension. Until Monday at 4 PM."

"To deposit $480,000?"

"No. To deposit $250,000. The requirement dropped because the stock recovered."

$250,000. Still more than I had liquid.

But not $480,000. Not total wipeout.

"What if I can't get $250,000?"

"Then Monday at 4 PM, we liquidate. But Olivia..." He paused. "Keller's involvement changes things. Big activists don't buy 10% positions on a whim. He sees value. The market will follow him."

"You're saying the stock could keep rising?"

"I'm saying it's possible. Monday morning, when the market opens, you'll see the real reaction. If it gaps up above $10, you're in the clear. No margin call. No liquidation."

If it gaps up above $10. If. So many ifs. But I wasn't dead. Not yet. Not today.

"Thank you," I whispered.

"Don't thank me yet. You're not out of danger. You're jus t... not dying tomorrow."

He hung up. I sat there. Grace in my lap. Laptop open. The stock was at $7.58 now. Still moving. I'd gone from losing everything to possibly surviving. In four hours. Because a stranger bought 10% of the company. Because David Keller saw the same value I did. Made the same analysis. Came to the same conclusion. And told the world.

Linda came into the kitchen. Saw my face.

"What happened?"

"An activist investor just bought 10% of the company. The stock jumped from $5.20 to $7.58 in after-hours trading."

She stared at me. "What does that mean?"

"It means I have until Monday. It means if the stock stays up, the margin call might be canceled. It means I might not lose everything."

Might. Maybe. If. Grace climbed down from my lap. Went to Linda. "Mama crying?"

I was crying. Didn't realize until Grace said it. Not sad crying. Not happy crying. Just... release. Linda picked Grace up. Looked at me.

"You're not safe yet."

"I know."

"You got lucky. Impossibly lucky."

"I know."

"Don't mistake luck for skill. Don't think this means you were right to gamble everything."

I nodded. Couldn't speak. She took Grace upstairs. Bath time. Bedtime routine. I sat alone at the kitchen table. Watching the after-hours ticker. $7.58 to $7.62 to $7.68. Still moving. Still climbing. But Richard was right. Monday morning would tell the real story. Monday would show if Keller's move was enough. If the market believed him. If I'd survive.

I didn't sleep that night either. Just lay in bed. Phone in my hand. Checking the price every few minutes. At 2 AM, my phone buzzed. Email notification.

From:dkeller@titancapital.com To:legal@ironjusticeholdings. comSubject: Carrington Media

I'll be brief. Titan Capital has acquired a 10% position in Carrington Media Group. We believe the company is deeply undervalued and mismanaged. We intend to pursue changes to leadership and strategy.

I understand Iron Justice Holdings owns 10.2% of the company. Together, we control 20%. That's enough to drive real change.

But I need to know whom I'm working with. Anonymous LLCs are fine for privacy, but partnerships require trust.

If you're interested in collaborating, you'll need to disclose your identity to my legal team.

Together, we have a real chance to unlock significant value. Are you ready for that?

Regards,

David KellerTitan Capital

I read it three times. Four times. David Keller. The man who dismantled CEOs for a living. The man who never lost. He didn't know who I was. Didn't know about the rape. Didn't know about Grace. Didn't know why I'd bought the stock. He just knew Iron Justice Holdings owned 10.2%. And he wanted to partner. To fight Tyler. To remove him as CEO. To destroy him.

My hands began to shake. But there was something else in the email. Something between the lines. He'd bought 10%

today. The same day I was about to be liquidated. The same day the stock hit $5.20.

Was that a coincidence? Or had he been the shark Richard mentioned? The unusual volume? The big buyer accumulating shares? Had Keller been watching? Waiting? Had he known about my position? About my margin call?

I didn't know. Couldn't know. But the timing was impossible to ignore. Grace stirred in her room. Made a sound through the monitor. Settled back into sleep.

I looked at the email again. The choice was clear. Stay anonymous. Stay hidden. Stay safe behind Iron Justice Holdings LLC. Hope the stock kept climbing. Hope I survived Monday. Or reveal myself. Join forces with Keller. Go to war openly. Risk everything again for the chance to actually win. But there was something Richard had said. Something that stuck in my head.

"Big activists don't buy 10% positions on a whim."

Keller had a plan. A strategy. Resources I didn't have. And he needed me. Needed my 10.2% to make his fight work. That meant I had leverage. That meant this wasn't just charity. I opened a reply email. Started typing.

Mr. Keller,

I'm interested.

My name is Olivia Parker. I'm the beneficial owner of Iron Justice Holdings LLC.

I bought 10.2% of Carrington Media Group because my analysis showed it was worth $60-70 per share. I'm still underwater on that position. Still fighting to survive a margin call.

I'm ready to fight. Ready to remove Tyler Carrington. Ready to unlock the value we both see.

But I need to understand something first. Your timing saved my position from a margin call. Probably saved my life. Was that coincidence? Or did you know?

And either way, what's this partnership going to cost me?

Best regards,

Olivia ParkerIron Justice Holdings LLC

I hit send before I could second-guess it. Closed the laptop. I went to check on Grace. She was sleeping, peaceful and unaware that Mama had almost lost everything, that a stranger had saved us, and that I was about to make another bet.

I whispered to her in the darkness, "I almost lost everything. But I'm still here. We're still here. Linda's right; I got lucky. Impossibly lucky. And luck doesn't mean I was right to gamble everything."

Grace stirred, made a small sound, and settled back into sleep. I returned to my room and lay down on my bed. After sending the email to Keller, I couldn't sleep; I just lay there watching the ceiling.

What had I just agreed to? David Keller. Legendary activist investor. The man who destroyed CEOs for a living. Worth $4.2 billion. And he wanted to fight beside me. Against Tyler. Against Margaret. Against a family with unlimited resources and no conscience.

My phone sat on the nightstand, screen dark, waiting for his response. Would he accept my questions? Would he tell me the truth about his timing? Or would he withdraw, deciding I was too damaged, too risky, too complicated?

The broken compass on my nightstand, Dad's compass, still spun, still lost. I avoided looking at it because I no longer knew my direction. I didn't know if I was making the right choice or if partnering with Keller was wisdom or just another form of revenge addiction.

My phone buzzed with an email notification: 3:47 AM.

From:dkeller@titancapital.com

Olivia,

I didn't know about your margin call specifically, but I knew someone was in trouble. The volume patterns suggested a large position under pressure. When I saw the Iron Justice Holdings 13D filing, I knew it was you.

I bought it because the price was right, because the company is deeply undervalued, and because I saw an opportunity.

But I'd be lying if I said your timing didn't matter. I'd be lying if I said I didn't know that showing up today would save your position.

Call it strategy, call it timing, call it whatever you want.

But yes, I knew. And yes, I acted deliberately.

As for what this costs you: everything and nothing.

My team will call you Monday morning. We'll need complete transparency about your financial position, your analysis, and your motivations. We'll need to structure this partnership carefully. There will be legal fees, compliance costs, and strategic requirements.

And here's what most people don't tell you about activist campaigns: they're expensive and slow. This fight could take *six months, a year, or could cost you more margin calls, more pressure, and more pain before it pays off.*

I can guarantee you'll stay in the fight. I can provide liquidity support, legal protection, and strategic resources. But I can't guarantee you'll win, that the stock will go up, or that this will end well.

I can only guarantee that if you partner with me, you'll have the best chance of winning that anyone in your position could have.

The question is: are you willing to pay the price? Are you willing to reveal yourself? Are you willing to bet everything again on this fight?

Because that's what this takes. Everything.

Think about it. Monday morning, you'll need to decide.

Regards,

David KellerTitan Capital

I read it twice. I felt sick. He was right. This would cost everything. Again. More stress. More risk. More time away from Grace. More broken promises. More chances to fail. But he was also offering something I didn't have: resources, strategy, protection, a chance to actually win. Not just survive. Win.

I looked at the ceiling and thought about Linda's words.

"Don't mistake luck for skill. Don't think this means you were right to gamble everything."

She was right. But maybe luck was the universe giving me one more chance. One more chance to choose: revenge or Grace, power or peace, winning or surviving.

I closed my eyes and listened to Grace breathing through the monitor. And I realized something. I still wanted to fight. I still wanted to see Tyler fall. And that terrified me more than the margin call ever had. No matter the cost. No matter who I hurt. No matter what I destroyed. I was my father's daughter after all. Just a different addiction. Same disease.

Grace made a sound through the monitor. Soft. Peaceful. And I knew what I'd choose on Monday. I knew it before Keller even asked. I knew it the moment I bought the stock. I'd choose revenge. Every single time. And Grace would pay for it. Just like Leo and I paid for Dad's choices. The pattern repeating. Generation after generation. Until someone was strong enough to stop. But that someone wasn't me. Not yet. Maybe not ever.

Chapter Two

The Ally

MONDAY, 6:00 AM. I woke before the alarm. Heart pounding. Mouth dry. Grace was still asleep. Linda too. I went downstairs, made coffee, and opened my laptop.

Futures markets were already trading. Premarket indicators showed CMG at $10.35, up from Friday's after-hours close of $7.68. But premarket didn't matter. Real volume happened at 9:30 AM. Real price discovery. That's when I'd know if Keller's thesis held, if the market believed him, and if I survived.

I sat at the kitchen table, watching the premarket numbers flicker. Linda came down at 7:15 AM. She saw me at the table, saw the laptop.

"How bad is it?"

"Premarket is up. But that doesn't mean anything until 9:30." She poured coffee and sat down across from me.

"What do you need?" The question surprised me. "What?"

"What do you need from me right now? Do you want me to distract you? Sit with you? Leave you alone?"

My throat got tight. "Sit with me. Please." She nodded, sipped her coffee, and said nothing. We sat in silence, watching the premarket numbers and the clock.

Grace woke at 8:00 AM. Linda got her, brought her down, and made her breakfast. Grace climbed onto my lap. Warm. Heavy. Real.

"Mama sad?"

"Mama's okay, baby. Just thinking."

"'Bout what?"

"About work stuff. Boring grown-up things."

9:00 AM. Thirty minutes until market open. My hands were shaking. Linda saw.

"Do you want to take Grace upstairs? Get away from the screen?"

"I can't. I have to watch."

"Then, Grace and I will sit with you." She moved her chair next to mine, Grace between us, the three of us watching the laptop. Grace didn't understand what we were looking at, but she knew it was important.

"What's that, Mama?"

"That's numbers, baby. They tell us if something good or bad happened."

"Good or bad?"

"We don't know yet. We're waiting to find out." She nodded, serious. "Waiting is hard."

"Yeah, baby. Waiting is hard."

9:15 AM. Fifteen minutes. Premarket was at $10.50 now, above my purchase price. But still not enough volume to matter. My phone buzzed. A text from Richard, my banker.

"Watching with you. Whatever happens, you fought hard. You should be proud of that."

I stared at the text, felt tears coming, and pushed them back. Not yet. Not until I knew.

9:29 AM. One minute. The screen showed the opening auction. Bids and offers were coming in. Price discovery was happening in real time.

Bid: $10.85, Offer: $11.20, Imbalance: 450,000 shares to buy

More buyers than sellers. Pressure building. My heart was pounding so hard I could hear it. Grace looked up at me. "Mama scared?"

"A little bit, baby."

"Count to four!"

She held up four fingers. "One, two, free, six!" I smiled despite everything. "One. Two. Three. Four."

"Feel better?"

"Yeah. I feel better."

9:30 AM. The market opened. The screen flashed. Opening price: $11.45. Price ticking: $11.45... $12.10. Up 49% from Friday's after-hours close. Up 14.5% from my purchase price. I stared at the screen. Couldn't breathe. Couldn't process.

Linda squeezed my hand tighter. "Olivia? Is that good?" I nodded. Tried to speak. Couldn't. Refreshed my brokerage account.

Margin Call: NONE

None. No margin call. No liquidation. No losing everything. I was above my purchase price. In profit. Safe. The relief hit me like a wave. I put my head in my hands. Started shaking.

"Olivia?" Linda's voice was anxious. "Talk to me."

"I'm okay." The words came out choked. "The margin call is gone. I'm safe." Linda pulled me into a hug. Grace was between us. Both of them were holding me.

"Thank God," Linda whispered. "Thank God."

I was crying. Couldn't help it. Five days of terror releasing all at once. From $5.20 to $12.10. From losing everything to being in profit. From bankruptcy to safety in four days. Because David Keller bought 10%. Because he announced it publicly. Because the market believed him. I was saved. Again. But this time it wasn't luck. It was strategy. It was someone powerful seeing what I saw. Betting on the same thesis.

Grace wiped my face with her small hands. "Mama crying?"

"Happy crying, baby. Mama's okay now." She hugged my neck tightly. Then went back to drawing. Two stick figures under a sun. Safe. Together.

Linda was watching me. "You survived."

"I survived."

"And now Keller wants to partner."

"Yes."

"And you're going to say yes." I looked at Grace. At her drawing. At her face. At everything I'd almost lost.

"I have a call with him at 2 PM. I'll hear what he wants. Then I'll decide."

Linda stood up. Started clearing breakfast dishes. "You've already decided. You decided the second you saw that stock price. The second you realized you could win."

She wasn't wrong. But I didn't say it out loud. Just sat there. Watching the stock. Watching it climb. Volume flooding in. Two hundred million dollars of shares trading in the first hour. The market was buying Keller's thesis. Buying my thesis. We were right. Both of us. Together. And at 2 PM, I'd find out what that meant. The whiplash of the stock movement still didn't feel real.

I opened the conference call link at 1:58 PM and stared at the blank screen, waiting. At exactly 2:00 PM, the screen came alive.

Five people appeared: professional backgrounds, expensive offices. David Keller was in the center. Smaller than I'd imagined, maybe 5'8". White hair, sharp eyes. Sixty-seven but looked fifty. The kind of energy that made you sit up straighter. Behind him, I could see framed photos: handshakes with presidents, CEOs, power brokers. To his left was Miranda Lee, an Asian woman in her early forties, wearing a Stanford Law sweatshirt. No makeup, sharp features, sharper eyes. A clean, modern office with law books visible on shelves. Three others I didn't recognize, probably analysts. Men in suits. Forgettable.

"Ms. Parker." Keller's voice was crisp, East Coast, lacking warmth. "Congratulations on surviving Monday."

My stomach flipped. "Thank you."

"The stock opened strong, up 48%. The market believes my thesis, believes your thesis. That's the first battle won." He leaned forward. "But understand something: Austerlitz was won in a day. The Napoleonic Wars took twelve years. We're just beginning."

He spoke like that. Military analogies, historical references, like everything was a campaign.

"I received your email Friday night. My team has spent the weekend running background checks. We've learned most of your story: McKinsey employment, Peninsula Hotel incident, Tyler Carrington's connection, Margaret's involvement."

He paused. "Before we proceed, I need to hear it directly from you. If we're going to be partners, I need complete honesty. I need to know who you are, why you bought this company, what your connection is to Carrington Media Group. All of it."

My hands started shaking.

"Tell me your story, Ms. Parker. Start from the beginning."

I took a breath and tried to steady my voice. "Okay, it seems you've already found out my background, but let me tell you the details. Five years ago, I was homeless, living on the street after losing my job at McKinsey. I was fired because I had a breakdown at a Peninsula Hotel networking event. It went viral. Millions of views. My life was destroyed."

Keller was writing something, not looking at me, just listening.

"I ended up working in prostitution to survive at a truck stop outside Chicago. That's where I met Tyler Carrington." I paused. This was the hard part.

"He didn't know who he was picking up. He didn't know I used to work at McKinsey. To him, I was just another homeless prostitute. An easy target."

My voice steadied as I got through it. "He brought me to his apartment and drugged me. I couldn't move or speak properly."

Keller's pen stopped moving. He looked up.

"He tied me down with silk scarves and raped me while Bach played on his speakers. I was paralyzed. Aware. But unable to fight back."

Miranda Lee was writing now too. Fast. Precise notes. My throat was tight. Silence on the call. Heavy. Uncomfortable.

"When I woke up hours later, I had bruises on my wrists and neck. Hours were missing from my memory. I went to the hospital. Rape kit. DNA match. Police investigated. Prosecutor reviewed."

"But they couldn't file charges. Tyler's mother is Margaret Carrington, CEO of Carrington Media, worth billions. She had lawyers, investigators, power. The prosecutor said she believed me but couldn't get a conviction."

Keller was studying me now, really looking. "Did you know who he was when you got in his car?"

"No, not until weeks later when the detective told me. Tyler Carrington, Margaret Carrington's son."

"And you knew Margaret?"

My hands clenched. "She was at that Peninsula Hotel event where I had my breakdown. She watched me fall apart, watched security escort me out. Then, months later, she came into the Nordstrom where I was working. Recognized me. Made one phone call. Got me fired on the spot."

"She destroyed my life before her son ever raped me." I looked at the camera, at Keller's face. "Six weeks after the rape,

I found out I was pregnant. Tyler's daughter. I kept her. Her name is Grace. She's three years old."

Grace's name felt sacred, saying it out loud to strangers, like I was exposing her, putting her in danger.

"Margaret found out about Grace, came to my mother's house, and offered me two hundred thousand dollars to disappear and sign an NDA. To never speak about what Tyler did. To never bring Grace near their family."

My voice cracked. "I said no." I stopped, tried to breathe.

"Then three other women came forward, women Tyler had raped using the same method, same drug, same silk scarves."

Miranda looked up. "So there's a pattern. Four victims total."

She spoke like that. Precise. Data-driven. Legal terminology. Like she was building a case in real time.

"Yes," I said. "Four of us. The DA reopened the criminal case last year. Tyler was facing actual charges, real consequences."

"But Margaret made it go away. Paid each victim $2 million. The charges were dropped. The case disappeared."

"Tyler walked free, promoted to CEO of Carrington Media eight months later, rewarded for being a rapist."

My voice was shaking now, anger bleeding through.

"So I waited. And when Tyler's company crashed 99% because of fraud, I saw my chance."

"I spent six months studying Carrington Media, reading financial statements, building models, documenting everything."

"And I bought 10.2% of the company at $10 per share. Used borrowed money. Bet everything I had."

"Because I believed two things. One: the company was undervalued, worth $60-70 per share based on fundamentals. Two: I could use my ownership position to force Tyler out, remove him as CEO, and make him face consequences." I looked directly at Keller. "That's why I bought. Not just for money, but for the chance to walk into a boardroom someday and vote him out of his own company."

Keller was silent for a long moment, just looking at me, calculating, measuring. "Ms. Parker," he said finally, "in war, the most dangerous soldiers are the ones fighting for something personal. They're unpredictable and emotional. They make tactical errors because they care too much."

He leaned closer to the camera. "But they're also the ones who never quit, never surrender, and never accept defeat. They're the ones who win impossible battles because losing isn't an option."

"I think you're one of those soldiers."

I didn't know if that was a compliment or a warning. Miranda spoke up, her voice sharp and precise. "Ms. Parker, I need to understand the legal exposure here. Section 16(b) of the Securities Exchange Act requires disclosure within 10 days of acquiring more than 5% of a public company. You filed your 13D on February 15th, correct?"

"Yes."

"Good. That's compliant. But Tyler and Margaret can access that filing. They can see that Iron Justice Holdings LLC owns 10.2%. They can try to pierce the corporate veil and find out who you are."

She was typing while she talked, multitasking. "Delaware LLCs provide privacy but not perfect anonymity, especially against motivated adversaries with resources. Margaret has resources. She also has something more dangerous: she knows you exist. She just doesn't know you're you yet."

"What do you mean?" My chest felt tight.

"Margaret was at the Peninsula Hotel when you broke down. She fired you from Nordstrom. She offered you money to disappear. She knows about Grace." Miranda's eyes were sharp. "She doesn't know Olivia Parker bought 10.2% of her company. But the moment she connects those dots, you're in real danger."

Keller cut in. "Which is why we need to be strategic. Julius Caesar said, 'divide and conquer.' We're going to do the opposite. We're going to unite forces, combine our positions, and present a unified front." Another military reference, but this time it made sense.

"Together, we own 20.2% of Carrington Media," Keller continued. "That's enough to force a proxy fight, force a vote, and force real change. But only if we coordinate, only if we plan carefully."

"Here's what I'm proposing: you stay anonymous and work behind the scenes. I'll be the public face, the one Tyler and Margaret focus on. While they're busy fighting me, you'll be invisible, safe, gathering intelligence and building the case."

Miranda jumped in. "Statistically, proxy fights succeed 68% of the time when the activist controls 15% or more of the shares. At 20.2%, our odds are approximately 73%. But that assumes careful execution, no mistakes, and no emotional decisions."

She looked at me. "Can you do that? Can you be patient? Can you work in the shadows for six months while David fights publicly?" Six months. Half a year. Waiting. Watching. Invisible.

"Yes," I said. "I can do that."

"Even when Tyler's on TV defending himself? Even when Margaret attacks David in the press? Even when you want to scream the truth about what Tyler did to you?"

"Yes."

Miranda studied me. "Trauma survivors often experience triggers during high-stress situations. PTSD symptoms. Intrusive memories. Difficulty regulating emotions under pressure. Section 10(b) anti-fraud provisions require material accuracy in all public statements. If you're triggered and make an emotional statement that's legally problematic, it could tank the entire campaign." Her precision was brutal. But not unkind. Just factual.

"I'm sober for four years," I said. "I've learned how to manage my emotions. How to stay present. How to function under pressure."

"Good." Miranda made a note. "Because this will test that. Every single day."

Keller leaned back. "Here's the timeline. Phase One: Information gathering. I'll file a 13D amendment this week announcing my intent to seek board seats. That starts the clock. We'll have 60 days to prepare for the proxy fight."

"Phase Two: Building the coalition. We'll reach out to other shareholders. Institutional investors. Convince them Tyler is destroying value. That new leadership is necessary. Phase Three: The proxy fight itself. Public campaign. Media battle. Board elections. This is where wars are won or lost. Where Caesar crossed the Rubicon. No turning back. Phase Four: Victory. Tyler is removed. New CEO installed. Company restructured. Value unlocked. You and I both profit. Justice served."

He made it sound simple. Clean. Inevitable. But I knew better. I knew nothing about this would be easy.

"What do you need from me?" I asked.

"Your vote. Your 10.2% in our column. Legally binding proxy authorization. And your patience. Your invisibility. Your willingness to let me fight this publicly while you wait." Miranda added, "We'll need complete financial transparency. Your brokerage statements. Your margin agreement. Your LLC structure. My team will conduct full due diligence under attorney-client privilege. That's Rule 1.6 of the Model Rules of Professional Conduct, which protects the disclosure of client information."

Everything she said came with a citation. A legal foundation. Like she was building a fortress one brick at a time.

"Okay," I said. "When do we start?"

"Now." Keller's face was serious. "But before we proceed, I need you to understand the cost. Not just financially. Personally." He paused and looked right at me.

"This fight will take a minimum of six months. Maybe longer. During that time, Margaret will investigate me. Attack me. Smear me in the press. She'll hire private investigators. Dig into my past. Look for weaknesses."

"And eventually, she'll start looking into you too. Into Iron Justice Holdings. Into who owns it. She'll try to find you. Expose you. Use your story against us."

"We'll protect you as much as possible. But there's no guarantee. No perfect defense. At some point, you might be exposed. And when that happens, Tyler will know. Grace's father will know who you are. What you did. What you're trying to do to him."

The thought made my stomach turn.

"But here's the alternative: you walk away. Tyler stays CEO. Margaret remains in power. Nothing changes. And you spend the rest of your life knowing you had the chance to fight and chose safety instead."

He leaned forward. "Hannibal crossed the Alps because the Romans thought it was impossible. Everyone told him to turn back. He didn't. He won battles no one thought he could win. Not because he was reckless, but because he understood that some fights are worth the risk."

"This is one of those fights."

I sat there, thinking about Grace, about Linda's warning, about what this could cost. But I was also thinking about Tyler's face, about Margaret's threats, about four years of waiting for justice that never came.

"If I do this," I said slowly, "I need something from you."

"Name it."

"Promise me that if it starts to hurt Grace, if Margaret exposes her in the press, you'll help me walk away. You'll let me quit. No questions. No pressure."

Keller was quiet for a moment, then nodded. "Agreed. Grace's safety comes first. If we reach that point, we end it. You have my word."

Miranda added, "I'll draft a termination clause into the proxy authorization. The Exchange Act allows the revocation of proxy authority at any time before the shareholder meeting. You'll maintain the legal right to walk away. We'll document it at a 2.3% attorney fee on dissolution. That's standard for termination agreements of this complexity."

Everything came back to numbers with her: percentages, legal codes, frameworks. It should have felt cold. But instead, it felt solid. Reliable. Like she was building protections I didn't know I needed.

"Okay," I said finally. "I'm in. Tell me what happens next."

Keller smiled, the first time I'd seen it. "Next, you come to New York. We meet in person, sign agreements, and coordinate strategy. Two days maximum. Then you go home to Grace, and we begin."

Miranda pulled up a calendar. "I've scheduled 11 hours of meetings across Tuesday and Wednesday. We'll need to review financials, draft proxy materials, coordinate with outside counsel, brief you on SEC reporting requirements under Schedule 14A, and—"

"Miranda." Keller cut her off gently. "Two days. We keep it focused." She nodded. "Two days. I'll send the agenda."

The call ended at 3:47 PM. I sat alone in my room, laptop closed, heart racing. I'd just agreed to go to war. Agreed to six months of hiding and waiting. Agreed to risk Grace's safety for the chance at justice.

Was I insane? Probably. But I'd also survived the margin call, survived Monday's opening, survived four years of waiting for this chance. And now someone powerful believed in my thesis. Believed in the fight. Believed in me. That had to mean something.

That night, I told Linda. She was in the kitchen, making dinner. Pasta. Grace's favorite.

"I'm going to New York. Monday. Two days."

Linda's knife stopped mid-cut. "You said yes."

"Yes."

"Of course you did."

She went back to cutting vegetables. Sharp. Precise. Angry.

"I need you to watch Grace while I'm gone."

"Of course you do."

"Mom—"

"No." She turned, knife still in hand. "You don't get to explain this away. You don't get to make it sound reasonable. You're choosing revenge over your daughter. Again. Just like Thursday. Just like Friday. Just like every day for the last eight weeks."

"This is different—"

"How? How is it different?"

"Because Keller has resources. Strategy. Legal protection. Because working with him means I can stay home with Grace for the next six months. Because this is the smart way to fight."

Linda set the knife down. Hard. "The smart way to fight is not to fight at all. The smart way is to take your profit, sell your stock, come home, and be Grace's mother. Let Tyler destroy himself. Because he will. Men like him always do."

"But Margaret won't. She'll protect him. Cover for him. Keep him in power. Unless someone forces change."

"And that someone has to be you?"

"Yes."

"Why?"

The question hung heavy. I thought about the silk scarves. The Bach. The paralysis. The hours I couldn't remember. I thought about Margaret's face at the Peninsula Hotel. Her phone call at Nordstrom. I thought about Grace. About her FASD. About her heart surgery. About her father being a rapist.

"Because I'm the only one who can," I finally said. "I'm the only one with enough shares, enough motivation, enough understanding of what they've done. Because it has to be me."

Linda studied my face, looking for the lie, for the crack. "You're going to lose yourself in this," she said quietly. "Just like Dad lost himself in alcohol. You're going to become obsessed. Consumed. Absent. And Grace is going to pay for it."

"I'm going to be here. Home. With Grace. For six months. While Keller fights publicly."

"But you won't really be here. You'll be thinking about it constantly. Planning. Obsessing. Living in that war even if you're not fighting publicly."

She wasn't wrong. But I didn't say it out loud. Grace came into the kitchen, holding a drawing. Two stick figures under a sun.

"Look, Mama! Look!" I took it, studied it like it was the most important document in the world.

"That's beautiful, baby. Is that you and me?"

"Yeah! We happy!"

She climbed onto my lap. Warm. Solid. Real. Linda was watching. Her face said everything. Look at what you're risking. Look at what you might lose.

"I need to ask you something," Linda said. "And I need an honest answer."

"Okay."

"Why are you really doing this?"

"To make Tyler face consequences—"

"No. The real reason. Not the one you tell yourself. The real one."

I looked down at Grace. At her hair. At her small hands gripping my shirt.

"Because I'm tired of being powerless," I said finally. "Tired of feeling like I'm still that woman on his bed. Paralyzed. Watching. Unable to fight back." My voice cracked. "I need him to know I fought back. I need him to see my face someday and realize I won. I need that, or I'll never be free."

Linda poured water for tea and set the kettle on the stove. "You won't be free anyway," she said quietly. "Even if you watch him get fired. Even if you get everything you want. You'll still be the woman he raped. He'll still be Grace's biological father. None of that changes."

"But I'll have power—"

"Power over him won't make you powerful. It'll just make you someone who destroyed him. And then what? Then who are you?"

The question hung heavy. Grace was falling asleep in my lap, her breathing slowing, thumb in her mouth.

"I don't know," I whispered. "I won't know until it's over."

"That's what I'm afraid of."

The kettle whistled. Linda poured tea. Chamomile. The smell of comfort. She sat down across from me, Grace between us, now sleeping.

"I'll watch Grace while you're in New York," Linda said. "But I need you to promise me something."

"What?"

"Promise me that no matter what happens, no matter how this turns out, you won't drink. That you'll stay sober. That you'll keep showing up for Grace even when you're distracted."

"I promise."

"Say it like you mean it."

"I promise I won't drink. I promise I'll stay sober. I promise Grace comes first even when revenge is screaming louder."

Linda studied my face for a long time. "Okay," she said finally. "Good. Then we understand each other." She stood, took her tea, and left the kitchen.

I sat alone, Grace sleeping in my lap, warm, heavy, peaceful. I whispered to her, "I'm going to fight for us. But I'm going to do it smart this time. I'm going to be patient. I'm going to come home to you. And when it's done, you'll have power he can never touch." She didn't answer. Just slept. And somewhere in the darkness, I thought I heard Leo's voice. Not a hallucination. Not a ghost. Just a memory.

You were always the smart one, Livvy. The one who knew how to plan, how to wait, how to win. Don't lose yourself in the waiting.

I promised him I wouldn't. But I wasn't sure I could keep that promise.

Chapter Three

4 AM Tears

GRACE WOKE UP CRYING at 4 AM Monday morning. Not her usual wake-up sounds. Crying. Hard. Like she knew something was wrong. I went to her room. She was sitting up in bed, face red, tears streaming. Her weighted blanket was tangled around her legs.

"Mama going 'way?"

My chest tightened. She knew. Somehow, she always knew.

"Just for two days, baby. Mama will be back Wednesday."

"No!" Her hands grabbed at the air between us, reaching. "No go, Mama!"

I sat on her bed. She climbed into my lap immediately, arms around my neck, holding on tight. Like if she held hard enough, I couldn't leave.

"I have to go, sweetheart. But Grandma will be here. And Mama will call you every day. And I'll be back so fast—"

"No fast!" She pulled back to look at my face, tears on her cheeks. "You go long time!"

She couldn't say it exactly right, but she understood. Time was long when I was gone.

"Two sleeps. That's all. One sleep, two sleep, then Mama's home."

"Two sleep?" She held up fingers, got it wrong. Three fingers instead of two. "This much?"

"Two." I gently folded down one finger. "Like this."

"'Kay." But her voice was small. Unsure. She'd heard promises before.

Linda appeared in the doorway, hair messy from sleep, face sad.

"It's 4 AM," she said quietly. "Your flight's not until 9. Let me take her."

"She wants me."

"I know. But you need to shower, pack, and get ready. I'll handle this."

Linda sat on the other side of the bed and held out her arms. "Come here, Gracie-girl. Let's let Mama get ready."

Grace looked between us, torn. Then she buried her face in my shoulder. "No. Want Mama."

"I know, baby." Linda's voice was gentle but firm. "But Mama needs to get ready for her trip. Come snuggle with me." She reached over and started rubbing Grace's back in slow circles, the way that usually calmed her. Grace's grip on me loosened, just slightly.

"That's it," Linda said. "Come here, sweetheart."

She took Grace from my arms. Grace whimpered but didn't fight. Too tired. Too overwhelmed. Linda settled her against her chest, started rocking, and began humming the lullaby she used to sing to me when I was small. When Dad was drunk and the world was scary. No words this time. Just the melody. Soft and low. Grace's breathing started to slow, her body growing heavy against Linda. Not sleep, just exhaustion. Resignation.

I stood there watching, my daughter being comforted by someone else. Because I was leaving. Because revenge mattered more than being here. Linda looked at me over Grace's head. Her eyes said everything her mouth didn't.

You're doing this to her. You're choosing this.

"Go," she said quietly. "Get ready. I've got her."

I went to my room, closed the door, and sat on my bed in the dark. What was I doing? Flying to New York to sign agreements with a billionaire to destroy Tyler. Leaving Grace for two days. Starting a war that would consume the next six months. For what? For power over Tyler? For the satisfaction of watching him lose? Was that worth this? Worth Grace's tears? Worth Linda's judgment? Worth risking everything again? I didn't know. But I was going anyway.

My phone was on the nightstand, flight confirmation glowing on the screen. **Flight 847 to LaGuardia. Departs 9:15 AM.** I had five hours. Five hours before I walked away from my daughter to chase revenge. I should cancel. Should stay. Should choose Grace. But I didn't reach for the phone to cancel. I reached for my suitcase instead.

Business class was wasted on me. Leather seat. Extra legroom. Free drinks I wouldn't touch. Four years sober. Wasn't starting now. The flight attendant kept asking if I needed anything: water, juice, a warm towel. I didn't need their attention, but I didn't say that.

The plane took off, Columbus disappearing below. Grace getting smaller. Further away. I closed my eyes, tried to sleep, but couldn't. Just saw Tyler's face. The way he'd looked at me that night. Empty eyes. Clinical. Like I was an experiment. Saw Margaret's face at Nordstrom, recognizing me. The pleasure in her eyes when she got me fired.

I opened my eyes. The woman next to me was reading a magazine, Business Insider. Cover story about activist investors. David Keller's face on the cover: "The Man Who Makes CEOs Sweat."

The woman noticed me staring. "You know him?"

"I'm about to."

She looked impressed. "He's brilliant. Ruthless. But brilliant. If he's targeting your company, you're either about to get very rich or very fired."

"What if I'm neither? What if I'm just along for the ride?"

She smiled. "Nobody's just along for the ride with David Keller. He doesn't take passengers. Only partners or enemies. And you don't want to be his enemy."

She went back to her magazine. I stared out the window. Partners or enemies. No middle ground. No safe position. I'd chosen partner. Now I had to live with what that meant.

LaGuardia Airport smelled like coffee and desperation. I'd never been to New York before. Not like this. Not for real. Exhaust. Garbage. A million people living too close together. Ambition thick enough to choke on. Everything felt bigger here. Faster. Like the city itself was moving and I needed to keep up or get crushed.

Walking through the terminal made my chest tight. All these people rushing somewhere important, looking like they belonged. I didn't belong. I was a girl from Ohio who'd spent time on the streets. Who'd survived things that should've broken me. But I was here anyway. In New York. My hands were sweating. I wiped them on my jeans. The last few years had taught me something: nothing was safe. Nothing was guaranteed. Power and money were the only things that mattered. And I'd learned to use both.

A driver was waiting with a sign that had my name. Black car. Tinted windows. I took a breath and walked toward him.

"Ms. Parker? I'm James. Mr. Keller sent me."

Professional. Polite. The kind of service money bought. The car was spotless. New car smell. Leather seats. Bottled water in the cupholder. I sat in back, watching the city pass.

Buildings getting taller. Denser. The skyline I used to dream about when I was at McKinsey. When I thought this city meant success.

James drove in silence. Didn't ask questions. Just navigated traffic like it was choreographed. We pulled up to a building on 57th Street. Glass. Steel. Expensive. The kind of building where people made decisions that changed lives.

"Mr. Keller's expecting you. 42nd floor. Miranda will meet you in the lobby."

I got out and looked up. The building stretched into the gray sky, clouds moving fast. Wind cold.

February in New York. Felt like punishment. Inside, the lobby was marble. Polished. Everything gleaming. Security desk. Turnstiles. The architecture of power.

Miranda Lee was waiting by the elevators, hair in a ponytail. She looked like a grad student except for her eyes. Sharp. Calculating. Missing nothing.

"Ms. Parker. Good flight?"

"Fine."

"Good. Let's go. David's waiting."

The elevator was fast and silent. My ears popped at the 30th floor. Miranda didn't notice, just checked her phone, typing something.

"Ground rules before we go in," she said without looking up. "David doesn't do small talk. He doesn't care about your feelings. He cares about whether you can help him win. So when he asks you questions, answer directly. No emotion. No backstory unless he asks. Just facts."

"Okay."

"And don't be intimidated by the office. He designs it to intimidate. That's the point."

The elevator opened on the 42nd floor. The reception area had glass walls and city views. You could see Central Park from here. See everything. Like the whole city was laid out for judgment.

A receptionist barely looked up, just waved us through. Miranda led me down a hallway. More glass. More views. Offices with closed doors. People in expensive suits moving fast. Titan Capital. The company that made CEOs sweat. That destroyed careers. That won 11 out of 14 proxy fights. And I was about to become their partner.

Miranda stopped at a door, knocked once, and didn't wait for an answer. Just opened it.

"She's here."

David Keller's office was exactly what Miranda said. Designed to intimidate. Wall of windows. Manhattan spread out below. Expensive furniture. Art I didn't recognize but knew cost more than my childhood home. And photos everywhere. Photos of Keller with people I recognized: presidents, CEOs, senators. People with power. People who'd been destroyed or elevated depending on whether Keller wanted them that way.

Keller stood at the window, looking out. Small man. White hair. Sharp suit. He didn't turn around immediately. Just kept looking at the city, making me wait.

"Ms. Parker." Finally, he turned. Those eyes. Sharp. Cold. Evaluating. "You made it."

"Yes."

"Good. Sit."

He gestured to a chair. I sat. Miranda sat beside me, pulling out a tablet. Keller stayed standing, positioned by the window, backlit, making himself hard to read. Miranda pulled out documents. Thick. Legal. Pages and pages.

"This is the partnership agreement. Titan Capital and Iron Justice Holdings. Joint proxy fight. Coordinated strategy. Shared decision-making on major moves. But David has final say on timing and tactics."

She flipped through pages and pointed to sections.

"You're agreeing to stay anonymous, to work through representatives, and to not file anything that reveals your identity without David's approval. That's non-negotiable."

"You're also agreeing that if we win, you get a board seat. 10% ownership guarantees that. But you serve at David's discretion. If he thinks you're a liability, you resign. That's in here too." More pages. More terms. More ways I was giving away control.

"And finally, if we lose, if shareholders vote against us, you pay half the campaign costs. That's roughly $1 million. You'd owe $500K. Can you afford that?"

My stomach dropped. "If we lose, the stock stays low and I need to pay half the campaign costs?"

"Yes, so we better win," Keller said. "Sign it."

Miranda handed me a pen. Expensive. Heavy. The kind that cost more than most people's monthly salary. I stared at the signature line. This was it. Point of no return.

If I signed, I was committed. Invisible partner in a proxy fight. Betting everything on removing Tyler. Risking Grace's stability. Risking Linda's trust. Risking everything I'd rebuilt. If I didn't sign, I flew home, kept my 10% position, hoped the stock recovered, stayed powerless, and let Tyler win. I thought about Grace's face this morning, crying. "Mama, no go." I thought about Tyler's face. Empty. Clinical. Counting to forty-seven.

I signed. Miranda witnessed it. Keller signed. It was done.

"Welcome to the war, Ms. Parker," Keller said.

I walked out of that conference room a different person than when I walked in. The girl who'd been homeless, who'd survived on the streets, who'd clawed her way back from nothing. She was gone. In her place was someone harder. Someone willing to sacrifice everything for revenge. I'd just bet my daughter's future, my mother's trust, and all of my money on destroying a man who destroyed my life. The old Olivia would have been terrified. But the new one? She felt alive for the first time in years. The war had started. And I was all in.

Chapter Four

Broken Promise

T HE STRATEGY SESSION LASTED four hours. Keller's team presented everything. Every detail. Every tactic. Every move planned months in advance. They'd analyzed Carrington Media for weeks, knowing the business better than Tyler did. They understood the weak points, the scandals, and the places to attack.

"Tyler's made three major mistakes," one analyst said. His name was James. Young. Eager. MBA from Wharton. "The StreamMedia acquisition. The menswear line. Caldwell & Main department stores. Total value destroyed: $800 million."

Charts appeared: numbers and graphs showing the destruction.

"But that's just incompetence. What we're really focused on is fraud."

My attention sharpened.

"Blackwood Capital published a short report two weeks ago," James continued. "They're alleging accounting irregularities, including subscriber numbers that don't match and revenue recognition problems. The stock dropped 18% in one day."

I shifted in my seat, trying to keep my face neutral.

"The allegations are specific," James said. "Blackwood claims Carrington inflated subscriber counts by including canceled accounts. They also claim they recognized revenue too early on multi-year contracts and that the Stream-Media acquisition was marked up internally to hide losses."

Keller was watching me. "You've read the report?"

"Yes." My voice was steady. "I sent them the information."

The room went quiet.

"You what?" Keller leaned forward.

"I found the discrepancies months ago. The subscriber reconciliation between parent company and subsidiary filings didn't match. StreamMedia's purchase price increased by $40 million between the initial press release and the 10-K filing six months later. Revenue recognition on the menswear line violated GAAP standards."

James was staring at me. Everyone was staring.

"I documented everything and sent it to Blackwood anonymously. I figured a short seller report would do more damage than me going to the SEC directly."

"How did you..." Keller stopped. Started again. "How did you even know where to look?"

"I worked at McKinsey in corporate finance. Before everything fell apart, I knew how to read financial statements and how to find what companies don't want you to find."

I pulled out my phone and opened my notes. "The subscriber inflation is the easiest to prove. Carrington counts any account that's been active in the last 180 days as a current subscriber. The industry standard is 90 days. That inflates their numbers by approximately 2.3 million subscribers." I kept going. I couldn't stop now.

"The StreamMedia acquisition was marked up post-close. They paid $340 million, but six months later, the 10-K shows a purchase price of $380 million. The extra $40 million went to 'integration costs' and 'goodwill adjustment.' That's fraud. You can't change the purchase price after the deal closes."

"The menswear line revenue is even worse. They're booking entire contract values upfront when the cash comes in over 18 months. That violates ASC 606. Revenue recognition has to match delivery."

Keller was leaning back now, arms crossed, studying me.

"You found all this yourself?"

"Yes."

"Why didn't you tell us in the last call?"

"I wasn't sure you'd believe me."

James was typing frantically. "This is... Ms. Parker, this is an incredibly sophisticated analysis. Most hedge fund analysts would miss half of this."

"I didn't miss it." My hands were shaking now. "I spent months on this. Every night after Grace went to sleep. Building the case. Making sure it was airtight."

Keller's expression changed. Respect. Maybe even admiration.

"You've been planning this longer than we have."

"Yes."

"And you understand the business implications? The legal liability? The SEC exposure?"

"Tyler misled shareholders. That's securities fraud. The board has liability. The auditors have liability. Everyone who signed those filings has liability." I met his eyes. "It's not just incompetence. It's criminal."

Keller smiled. Actually smiled. "We're going to win this proxy fight."

"I know."

"But," Keller continued, "there's something else. Something bigger that we found."

Miranda pulled up new slides. "We've been investigating Carrington Media's historical operations. Pre-Tyler. Margaret's era."

My pulse quickened.

"Carrington Media owns a chain of nightclubs and entertainment venues. Acquired in 2014. Ostensibly as part of their lifestyle brand expansion. But the financials don't make sense."

My chest felt tight.

"The clubs operate at a loss. They have for years. But Carrington keeps them open. Keeps funding them. We couldn't figure out why until we started looking at the transaction patterns." Miranda clicked to the next slide. Lists of venues. Cities. My vision blurred for a second.

"The clubs process massive amounts of cash. Way more than their actual business justifies. And there are unusually high 'advertising buys' from shell companies. Hundreds of businesses paying inflated rates for club promotions that never actually run." She paused.

"It's money laundering. The clubs are washing cash for organized crime. Gang money. Drug money. We can't prove Margaret knows, but her company is facilitating it."

"Which gangs?" The words came out before I could stop them. My voice was too sharp. Too urgent. Keller looked at me. Surprised.

"We're still identifying all of them. Operations in six cities. Cleveland. Detroit. Milwaukee—"

"Cleveland." My hands were shaking. "Which areas in Cleveland?"

Miranda glanced at Keller. Something passed between them.

"East side primarily. One club called Club Vertical services several surrounding towns. Why?"

"What towns?" I couldn't breathe. "What surrounding towns?"

"Ms. Parker—"

"What towns?" My voice broke.

Miranda checked her notes. "Garfield Heights. Maple Heights. Bedford. And a smaller town called Millfield."

The room tilted. Everything went quiet. Like someone turned off the sound.

"That's where I'm from." My voice didn't sound like mine. "Millfield. That's where I grew up."

Keller sat forward. "You never mentioned—"

"My brother." The words felt like glass in my throat. "My brother Leo. He died in 2014. He owed money to a gang. Eight thousand dollars. They killed him."

Silence. Complete silence. Something flickered in the corner of my vision. A shape. A shadow.

Leo. Standing there by the window. Not moving. Not speaking. Just looking at me with those sad, sad eyes. The same eyes from the funeral. From every nightmare I'd had for seven years. He looked disappointed. Like I had failed him. Like I was still failing him.

"Ms. Parker." Keller's voice was careful. Gentle. "I'm sorry. We didn't know."

I blinked hard. Leo was still there. Solid. Real. Waiting.

"When did the money laundering start?" I forced the words out. "At that club. Club Vertical."

"2015." Miranda's voice was soft now. "Right after the clubs were acquired."

My throat was so tight I could barely speak. "Leo died in 2014."

"Different timeline," Keller said. "Your brother's death predates Carrington's involvement."

The shape flickered. Leo. Still watching. Still waiting for something from me. I didn't look at him. I kept my eyes on Keller. On the real people. On the ones who couldn't see what I was seeing.

"But the gang that killed him," I whispered. "Did they use those clubs?"

Keller exchanged a look with Miranda. "Yes," he said finally. "Starting in 2015. That's the only gang in that area. They used Club Vertical for money laundering. Grew significantly because of it. Became more organized. More powerful."

Leo's shape was there. Against the wall now. Not moving. Not talking. Just sad. My chest hurt. Like my ribs were breaking.

"The gang became bigger and more dangerous, partly because Margaret's clubs gave them infrastructure. A way to clean their money. A way to expand," Keller continued. His voice was steady. Professional. But kind.

I was shaking. Hands. Legs. Everything.

"So Margaret's company helped them." My voice cracked. "Helped the people who killed my brother become stronger."

"We can't prove a direct connection to your brother's death," Keller said carefully. "The timeline doesn't support it. But we can prove Margaret's company facilitated organized crime operations that killed dozens of people over the years."

Leo flickered. Faded slightly. Like he was losing strength.

"Why are you telling me this?" I couldn't stop shaking. "Are you going to use it in the proxy fight?"

"No." Keller's voice was firm. "We're going to use the fraud to remove Tyler. The securities violations. The subscriber inflation. The revenue recognition problems. That's clean. That's direct. That puts liability on the board."

"But the gang stuff—"

"Is Margaret's crime. Not Tyler's." Keller leaned forward. "Tyler committed fraud as CEO. Clear exposure. The board has to remove him, or they're all liable for shareholder lawsuits. That's our weapon. Fast. Certain. It wins us the proxy fight in six months."

"The gang operations, the money laundering, that takes years to prosecute. FBI investigations. Grand juries. If we try to use that to remove Tyler now, Margaret's lawyers will bury it. Delay everything. The proxy fight would drag on forever."

My vision was blurring. Tears. Anger. I couldn't tell.

"So we separate the battles," Keller continued. His voice was gentle but unyielding. "We use fraud to destroy Tyler. Remove him as CEO. Destroy his reputation. End his career. That's your revenge on him. That fight, we do together."

He paused and looked at me directly.

"But the second fight... the criminal case against Margaret for money laundering... that's not our business. We're an activist hedge fund. We fight proxy battles. We don't prosecute federal crimes."

Leo was there. Solid again. Looking at me. Waiting for my answer. I wanted to scream. Wanted to demand they handle everything. Wanted someone else to carry this weight. But Keller was right. Leo was my brother. This was my fight.

Leo's shape flickered. Faded. Gone. I let out a breath I didn't know I was holding. "I understand." My voice was breaking. "One fight together. One fight alone."

"Exactly." Keller stood. "That's enough for today. You're staying at the Peninsula. Titan's paying. A car will take you. Rest. Tomorrow we meet with the legal team. Wednesday you fly home."

I stood. My legs were unsteady. The room was spinning. Too much information. Too many revelations. Too many ghosts.

Miranda walked me to the elevator. "You okay?"

"I don't know." My voice sounded hollow. Empty.

"The Leo connection... I'm sorry. We didn't know."

"He died in 2014." I was barely holding it together. "Margaret's clubs came after. But knowing they helped those gangs grow. Knowing her money made them stronger..."

"Makes it personal. I understand." Miranda pressed the elevator button. "But Ms. Parker? Don't let personal cloud business. We win the proxy fight first. Then you get justice for your brother. In that order. Can you do that?" The elevator opened.

Could I do that? Could I wait six months while Margaret walked free? While the woman whose company helped arm my brother's killers kept living her life?

"Because if you can't," Miranda continued, "if you're going to get emotional and reckless, tell me now. Before we're too deep to back out."

I thought about Leo. About how he died calling my name. About how I couldn't save him. About how I'd spent seven years carrying that failure.

"I can do it." My voice was steadier now. "I can be patient."

"Good. See you tomorrow. 9 AM. Don't be late."

I stepped into the elevator. The doors closed. I was alone. I leaned against the wall. Let the tears come. Leo's face was there. Behind my eyelids. Sad. Disappointed. Waiting.

"I'm trying," I whispered to the empty elevator. "I swear I'm trying. I'll make it right. I'll make them pay. Both of them." My voice broke.

"I'm sorry I couldn't save you. But I can do this. I can finish this."

The elevator descended. Taking me back down. Back to street level. Back to the city that had destroyed me once already.

The Peninsula Hotel was where it started. The night I'd screamed about Leo in front of three hundred people. The night the viral video began. The night Margaret Carrington had watched me collapse. Different Peninsula. This was New York. That was Chicago. But the same chain. Same luxury. Same marble floors and crystal chandeliers and the smell of money.

Walking into the lobby felt like stepping into a memory I couldn't escape. My room was on the 23rd floor. City views. King bed. Marble bathroom. Everything felt expensive and sterile. I stood at the window looking out. Manhattan at night. Lights everywhere. People everywhere. Moving. Living. Not paralyzed by the past. I was reaching for my phone to call Grace when it buzzed.

Text from Miranda: "Can you come down to the lobby? Need to discuss something." My stomach tightened. What now? What else could there possibly be?

I took the elevator back down. Miranda was waiting in a corner of the lobby, away from people. Private.

"What's wrong?"

"Nothing's wrong." She gestured to a chair. "Sit, please." I sat, my heart pounding.

"Keller was impressed with you today. Your analysis of the fraud. The way you found the discrepancies. The depth of your understanding of the business."

"Okay."

"He wants you to stay in New York. Work with the team. Help us build the case against Tyler. Your knowledge of Carrington Media is unparalleled. You see things we miss."

My chest tightened. "For how long?"

"Six months. Until the proxy vote. You'd work directly with our analysts. Full access to everything. You'd be part of the strategy team."

Six months. Six months away from Grace. "I can't."

Miranda leaned forward. "Ms. Parker—"

"I promised my daughter I'd be home Wednesday. I told her two more sleeps. She's three years old. I can't just disappear for six months."

"We'd compensate you. Significantly—"

"No." My voice was firm. "I can't. I won't do that to Grace."

Miranda was quiet for a moment, studying me. "What if it was one month? Not six. Just one month to help us build the foundation. Get the initial strategy locked down. Then you could go home and work remotely."

One month. Thirty days. Four weeks away from Grace. "I can't."

"We'd pay you $50,000 for the month. Plus all expenses. Plus a first-class flight home when the work is done. You could FaceTime Grace every day. After the month, you'd still be involved, but from home."

Fifty thousand dollars. More money than I'd made in years. Money I could put toward Grace's future. Toward stability. Toward everything we needed.

"And," Miranda continued, "you'd have complete access to everything we find about the clubs. About the money laundering. About the gangs. You want to build a case against

Margaret? You need resources. Information. Connections. We can provide that."

Leo's face flashed in my mind. Sad eyes. Waiting. One month to help destroy Tyler. One month to get the information I needed to go after Margaret. One month away from Grace.

"I need to think about it."

"Take the night. But Ms. Parker? This is how you win. Not by yourself. Not alone. You need help. Resources. A team. We're offering that."

She stood. "Text me in the morning. If you say yes, we'll start Wednesday. If you say no, you fly home, and we do this without you."

She walked away, leaving me sitting there in the lobby of the Peninsula Hotel, where everything had started to fall apart. And now I had to choose again: Grace or revenge, present or power, mother or warrior. I went back to my room, my chest tight.

My phone buzzed. FaceTime. Linda. I answered. Grace's face filled the screen. "Mama!"

"Hi, baby! I miss you so much!"

"Miss you!" She was in her blue pajamas. "When you come home?"

My throat tightened. "Wednesday. Two more sleeps. That's all." But was that true? Was I coming home Wednesday, or was I about to break another promise?

"Promise?"

The word hit like a punch.

"I..." I couldn't finish.

Linda's face appeared beside Grace. She saw my expression and immediately knew something was wrong. "Grace, sweetie, go pick out a book for bedtime. I'll be right there."

"Okay!" Grace ran off.

Linda's face moved closer to the screen. "What happened?"

"They want me to stay one more month. To help with the strategy. They'll pay me fifty thousand dollars."

Linda's expression hardened. "One month? You told Grace two days. TWO DAYS, Olivia."

"I know, but—"

"No." Linda's voice was icy. "Absolutely not. You promised her. You looked at her face this morning, and you promised two sleeps. And now you're going to break that promise for money?"

"It's not just money. Mom, listen. Keller's team has been investigating Margaret. Not just Tyler. They found things. About the clubs. About gang operations in Cleveland."

Linda went very still. "What kind of things?"

"Margaret's nightclub in Millfield, Club Vertical. It was laundering money for gangs, starting in 2015. They have financial records and evidence of organized crime operations."

"What does that have to do with Tyler?"

"Nothing. That's Margaret's separate criminal enterprise. But Keller's team found it while investigating the company." I took a breath. "Mom, the gangs they were funding were in Millfield—"

"No." Linda's voice was suddenly sharp, knowing. "Don't say it."

"The same gang that killed Leo used those clubs. After 2015, they became more organized and powerful. Margaret's infrastructure helped them grow."

The silence was deafening. I could hear Linda breathing, fast and shallow.

"Are you saying—" Her voice broke. "Are you saying Margaret Carrington's company helped fund the people who killed my son?"

"Yes."

Linda's hand covered her mouth, her eyes filling with tears. "Oh my God." She was shaking. "Oh my God, Olivia."

"The timeline doesn't prove a direct connection to Leo's death. He died in 2014, and the club operations started in 2015. But the gang network was already there, and Margaret's money made them stronger."

"Do you have proof?" Her voice was barely a whisper. "Real proof?"

"Keller's team has evidence. Financial records. Money trails. Enough to potentially build a federal RICO case against Margaret. But I don't have access to it yet."

"What do you mean 'yet'?"

I swallowed hard. "That's the offer. If I stay one month to help them build the case against Tyler. That's what they need me for: the fraud analysis. Then after, they'll give me complete access to everything they've found about Margaret's criminal operations. All the evidence. All the connections. Everything."

"And the fifty thousand dollars?"

"That's for the month of work on Tyler's case, the proxy fight, removing him as CEO."

Linda wiped her face with trembling hands. "So you'd stay one month working on Tyler. And then they'd give you the information about Leo?"

"Yes. They're separating the cases. Tyler's corporate fraud is fast. They can take him down in six months through a proxy fight. Margaret's criminal enterprise will take years. FBI investigations. Federal prosecutors. They can't do both at once."

"But they'll give you the evidence about the gangs?"

"Everything they have, so I can work with federal investigators myself. Build a case for Leo."

Linda closed her eyes and took a long breath. When she opened them, they were wet and red. "Grace needs you," she said quietly.

"I know."

"She's three years old. She doesn't understand Tyler or proxy fights or any of this. She just knows her mama keeps leaving."

"I know that too."

Silence stretched between us. I watched Linda's face and saw something working in her, something tearing her apart from the inside. She looked away from the camera, down at her hands. When she spoke again, her voice was so quiet I almost couldn't hear it.

"Leo died alone." The words fell like stones.

"Shot and left behind a warehouse. And no one was ever held accountable. The men who did it are probably still out there, still hurting people."

She pressed her palms against her eyes. Her shoulders shook.

"Mom—"

"Let me finish." She lowered her hands. Her face was devastated. "I've spent seven years not knowing, not having answers, not being able to get justice. Do you know what that does to you? Waking up every single day knowing your child was murdered and no one cared enough to find out why?"

"I know—"

"You don't know." Her voice cracked. "You have Grace. She's alive. She's here. You get to hold her. But Leo? All I have is his grave and questions. Always questions. Who really did it? Why? If they're still out there? If they hurt other people's sons too?"

She took a shaky breath. "If this is the only way to get evidence about Leo's death... if this is the only chance we'll ever have to find out who was really responsible—" She stopped and looked directly at me, tears streaming down her face.

"I can't believe I'm about to say this."

"Mom, you don't have to—"

"Yes, I do." Her voice was firmer now, but shaking underneath. "Because if I don't say it, you'll stay anyway. And then I'll spend the next month hating you for breaking Grace's heart. But if I say it... if I tell you it's okay, then at least... at least we're making this choice together."

She wiped her face roughly. "I don't want you to stay. I want to tell you to come home right now. To get on a plane and forget about Tyler and Margaret and all of it. To just be Grace's mother. That's what I want."

"Then I'll come home—"

"But I can't say that." Linda's face twisted. "Because Leo was my baby. My son. And if you walk away from this chance... this one chance to finally get answers about what happened to him, I don't think I could forgive you. Or myself."

"Mom—"

"So you stay." The words came out choked. "You stay one month. You work on Tyler's case. You get the information about Leo. And then you come home. That's the deal."

"Are you sure?"

"No." Linda's voice broke completely. "I'm not sure about anything. I hate this. I hate everything about this. But Olivia—" She looked at me directly. "I need to know. I need to know who killed my son. And if staying one month gets us that answer, then... then you have to do it."

She took a shaky breath. "But one month. Not six. Not two months. ONE MONTH. Do you understand me?"

"I understand."

"Because if you break this promise, if you stay longer, if you get sucked into the Tyler fight and forget about Grace—" Her voice went cold. Hard. "I will never forgive you. And I will choose Grace over you. I'll raise her myself if I have to."

"I won't break it. One month. Then, I come home with the evidence about Leo."

Linda pressed her hand to her forehead. Closed her eyes. "God help me. I'm choosing a dead child over a living one."

"That's not—"

"It is." She opened her eyes. "It is, and we both know it. I'm choosing Leo. Choosing answers about his death. Choosing closure. And Grace is the one who's going to pay for it."

She paused. Steadied herself. "Grace is coming back. And you're going to tell her something. Keep it simple. She's three. She won't understand most of it. But she'll understand you're staying. And that's what will hurt her."

"Should I even tell her why?"

"Yes." Linda's voice was firm but shaking. "You tell her about Uncle Leo. Keep it simple. Use words she knows. She won't understand everything, but she deserves the truth. Even if it's just... just the shape of it."

Grace appeared on screen behind Linda, book in hand. "Gamma! Book!" Linda turned, her voice immediately gentle despite the tears on her face. "Good job, sweetheart. Come here. Mama wants to talk to you."

"'Kay!" Grace climbed onto Linda's lap. She saw me on the screen. "Mama!"

"Hi, baby." My voice was shaking.

"Mama home?"

"Not yet, sweetheart. Mama needs to tell you something." Her face changed. She became cautious. She knew that voice. She sensed something bad was coming.

"What?"

I took a breath. How do you explain this to a three-year-old? "Remember Uncle Leo? Gamma's boy? He's in heaven?"

"Leo heaven." She said it like she'd heard it before but didn't really understand.

"Yes. And Mama found people who know things about what happened to Leo." Grace blinked. Not understanding but trying.

"Bad people hurt Leo," I said slowly. "And Mama's trying to find out who. So they get in trouble."

"Bad people?" Her voice got smaller.

"Yes. But Mama has to stay here a little longer to find out."

Her face started to crumple. "But... you said come home."

"I know, baby. Mama's sorry. It's going to be longer now."

"How long?" Her voice was breaking.

"One month. That's... that's a lot of sleeps."

"No!" The tears came fast. "Mama home NOW!"

"I can't, baby. I'm so sorry. But it's for Uncle Leo—"

"Don't care!" She was sobbing. "Want Mama! Mama come HOME!"

"I know you want Mama here—"

"Mama always goes!" She buried her face in Linda's shoulder. "Always goes!" Linda held her tight, rocking her. Grace's little body was shaking with sobs.

"Mama NO GO! NO GO!" Linda looked at me over Grace's head. Her face was shattered. Tears streaming. But her jaw was set.

"One month," she said quietly, having to raise her voice over Grace's crying. "You work on Tyler's case. You get the information about Leo. Then you come home."

"I promise."

Grace was still sobbing. "Mama... Mama..."

Grace's sobs were quieter now. Exhausted. Her thumb in her mouth. Face red and wet. Linda kissed the top of Grace's head, then looked at me. "Goodnight, Olivia. One month. Don't make me regret this more than I already do."

She hung up before I could say anything else. The screen went black. I could still hear her crying in my head. "Mama NO GO!" She was right. She needed me. And I was choosing to leave anyway. I texted Miranda: "I'll stay. One month. Starting Wednesday."

She responded immediately: "Good decision. See you Wednesday morning. 9 AM."

Good decision... I lay down, stared at the ceiling, and thought about calling Janet. My sponsor. The woman who'd told me I was addicted to chaos. But I didn't call. Because she'd tell me to stop, to go home, to choose Grace. And I'd just chosen Leo and Tyler instead. Both of them. The dead brother I couldn't save. The rapist I couldn't stop.

I told myself it was about justice. About finally getting answers for Linda. About making sure the people who killed Leo faced consequences. And it was. Part of it was. But the other part, the part that made my heart race, was Tyler. Being in that room when he fell. Watching him lose everything. Having a front-row seat to his destruction. I wanted both: justice for Leo and revenge on Tyler. And I was willing to break Grace's heart to achieve them.

Grace's voice echoed: "Mama always goes!" Because that was the pattern now. That was who I'd become. The mother who always left. Who always chose something else. Someone else. Always one more thing. One more fight. One more month.

Dad had always promised "just one more drink." I had just promised Linda, "just one more month."

Outside, Manhattan hummed. Alive. Indifferent. And somewhere in Ohio, Grace was crying. Linda was holding her, believing I'd come home. One month. I would come home. I had to. But sitting here in the dark, a small voice whispered: *Will there always be one more month?* I didn't know. And that terrified me more than anything else.

Chapter Five

From Millfield to Manhattan

I DIDN'T SLEEP. THE Peninsula Hotel bed was too soft. Too quiet. Too empty without Grace's breathing in the next room. I kept checking my phone: 2 AM, 3 AM, 4 AM, 5 AM. Nothing from Linda. Grace would be asleep now. Safe.

I showered at 5:30 and dressed in the clothes I'd brought: black pants and a white blouse. The uniform of competence. The armor I used to wear at McKinsey when I needed to be taken seriously. My reflection in the mirror looked hollow. Dark circles under my eyes. Hair pulled back too tightly. The face of someone who'd made a choice and couldn't take it back.

I'd grown up in Millfield, a small town in Ohio, with Dad drinking himself to death while Leo and I hid in the basement. I got out: Ohio State, McKinsey, Chicago. But then I was fired. Homeless. Working truck stops. Drinking vodka for breakfast. Dad died that way. I almost followed. But I didn't. Three years sober. Built Parker Media from nothing. And now I was back at the Peninsula. Same hotel brand. Different woman.

This time fighting the same billionaire instead of falling apart in front of her. A girl from Millfield who used to hide from her drunk father. Now owning 10% of Margaret Carrington's company. Now partnered with David Keller. The story didn't make sense. But I was here anyway.

Miranda's text arrived at 8:15 AM: *Car waiting downstairs. Titan Capital. 47th floor.* No turning back now.

The Titan Capital offices didn't feel real. Glass walls. City views stretching forever. Conference rooms with tables that probably cost more than Linda's house. Everything chrome, leather, and expensive. Young people everywhere. Moving fast. Talking into headsets. Staring at screens showing numbers I recognized: stock prices, trading volumes, portfolio values. This was power. Real power. The kind that moved markets and destroyed CEOs.

Miranda met me in the lobby. Same professional suit. Same sharp eyes. "Good morning. Ready?"

I wasn't. But I nodded anyway. She led me down a hallway, through glass doors into a massive conference room. Twelve people were already there, all looking at me.

"Everyone," Miranda said. "This is our fraud analyst. She's joining us for the month." No name. Just "fraud analyst." Anonymous. Invisible. The way Keller wanted it.

A young guy stood up. Mid-twenties. Eager face. "James Rodi. Wharton MBA. Lead analyst on the Carrington case." He gestured to the others. "Sarah Park, former SEC. Marcus Delgado, forensic accountant. The rest of the strategy team."

They all nodded. Professional. Curious. Wondering who I was and why Keller brought me in. "Let's get started," Miranda said.

The screens came alive. Tyler's face everywhere. In photos, in videos, in newspaper headlines. The man who'd raped me staring down from every wall. My chest tightened. But I forced myself to breathe. To stay present.

James pulled up a presentation. "We've been working on this case for three months. Here's where we are." Charts appeared: financial statements, subscriber data, revenue projections.

"Tyler's made three catastrophic acquisitions," James continued. "StreamMedia for eight hundred million. A menswear line for two hundred million. Caldwell and Main department stores for four hundred million. Total value destroyed: one point four billion."

Marcus leaned forward. "But that's just incompetence. What we need is fraud."

"Exactly." Sarah's voice was sharp. "Incompetence doesn't remove a CEO. But securities fraud? That gets board members sued. That creates liability. That forces their hand."

She pulled up another document. "Two weeks ago, Blackwood Capital published a short report alleging accounting irregularities. The stock dropped eighteen percent in one day."

My hands tensed. I was the one who did the analysis and sent it to Blackwood Capital anonymously.

"The allegations are specific," Sarah continued. "Inflated subscriber counts. Premature revenue recognition. Classic fraud indicators."

"But Blackwood didn't provide proof," Marcus added. "They just pointed at the numbers and said something was wrong."

James turned to me. "That's where you come in. Keller says you see things we miss. That you understand Carrington Media better than anyone."

All eyes were on me. I took a breath. "Can I see the last four quarterly filings?"

James pulled them up immediately. I studied the screens. Numbers I'd analyzed a dozen times before. But now, with access to their research, I saw new patterns.

"There," I said, pointing. "Q2 2024. They reported three point two million subscribers. But look at the churn rate disclosed in the footnotes."

Marcus squinted. "Twelve percent quarterly churn."

"Which means they lost three hundred eighty-four thousand subscribers that quarter. But they added five hundred thousand new subscribers to report a net growth of one hundred sixteen thousand."

Sarah frowned. "That's normal for subscription businesses."

"Yes. But look at Q3." I pulled up the next filing. "Reported subscriber count: three point three million. Net growth: one hundred thousand. But the churn rate dropped to eight percent."

James was writing fast. "That's unusual."

"It's impossible," I said. "Churn rates don't drop four percentage points in one quarter. Not without a massive retention program. And look at their expenses. No increase in customer spending. No retention initiatives disclosed."

Marcus was nodding now, starting to understand.

"They're lying about the churn rate," I continued. "They're keeping canceled subscribers in the active count longer than they should, making the numbers look better."

"Can you prove it?" Miranda's voice cut through.

"Not yet. But if we had access to their internal systems, we could compare reported subscribers to actual active accounts."

"We don't have that access," Sarah said.

"Then we need someone inside who does."

The room went quiet. Keller's voice came from the doorway. I hadn't heard him enter.

"We have someone inside."

Everyone turned. He walked to the head of the table. Calm. Controlled. The billionaire who never lost.

"Three days ago, someone from Carrington Media reached out to us. Anonymously. Through an encrypted email." He pulled up a message on the screen.

I work at Carrington Media Group. I've watched Tyler Carrington ruin this company for three years. I've seen him lie to investors, inflate numbers, and manipulate the books.

I can't stay silent anymore. I decided to send this email to you because your firm publicly announced a 10% position with the intention of removing Tyler as CEO. I align with your vision and goal.

I'm sending you proof: real subscriber data, internal audit reports, and emails showing Tyler knew the numbers were fraudulent.

Use it. Remove him before he destroys everything.

My heart was pounding.

"Is it legitimate?" Sarah asked.

"We had our cybersecurity team trace it," Keller said. "The email originated from Carrington Media's internal network. This person is real. They work there."

Marcus leaned forward. "What did they send?"

Keller nodded to James. James pulled up a spreadsheet. "Subscriber data for the last eight quarters. Real data, not the inflated numbers they report publicly."

I stared at the screen. Q2 2024: Reported subscribers: 3.2 million. Actual active subscribers: 2.7 million. Half a million fake subscribers. Q3 2024: Reported: 3.3 million. Actual: 2.6 million. The gap was growing.

"They're counting accounts that haven't logged in for six months," I said quietly. "Accounts that have been canceled but haven't been purged from the system. Dead accounts."

"And Tyler knows," Sarah said, reading another document. "Look at this email."

An email chain appeared on the screen.

From: Tyler Carrington To: Steve Adler (CFO) Subject: Q3 Numbers

Steve,

I don't care about the actual churn rate. I care about what the Street sees. Make the subscriber numbers look strong. That's your job.

TC

The room was silent.

"He's admitting it," James breathed. "He's instructing his CFO to commit fraud."

"When did the whistleblower send this?" I asked.

"Monday night," Keller said. "The night before you arrived."

The timing was perfect. Too perfect.

"Why now?" Marcus asked what I was thinking. "Why reach out now after three years?"

Keller's expression didn't change. "According to their message, the anonymous whistleblower saw Tyler ruin the company and observed me announce my position. They realized someone was finally fighting back."

"They want Tyler gone as much as we do."

I studied the email on the screen. The smoking gun we needed. But something felt off. "This is a corporate email system," I said. "IT can track everything. If Tyler wanted to hide fraud, he wouldn't use company email."

Sarah nodded slowly. "That's a good point."

"Unless he's arrogant," Miranda said. "Which we know he is."

"Or unless someone kept these emails specifically," Keller added. "Someone who wanted insurance, leverage, or protection."

The CFO, Steve Adler. The man Tyler was instructing to commit fraud.

"You think the whistleblower is the CFO?" James asked.

"Maybe," Keller said. "Or someone close to him. Someone with access to the company's email server."

"Either way," Miranda cut in, "we have what we need: direct evidence that Tyler knowingly inflated subscriber numbers. That's securities fraud. The SEC will investigate. The board will have to act."

She turned to me. "Can you verify these numbers? Make sure the internal data is consistent with what we know about the business?"

I could. That's what I was good at: finding patterns, spotting lies.

"Yes."

"How long?"

"Three hours. Maybe four."

Keller nodded. "Do it. This is our case. This is what removes Tyler."

The meeting broke, people scattering to their desks, their screens, their phones. I sat there looking at Tyler's email. *I don't care about the actual churn rate. I care what the Street sees.* Two sentences that would destroy him. Two sentences from an anonymous whistleblower who appeared exactly when we needed them. It should have felt like victory. Instead, it felt like standing on ice, hearing it crack, not knowing when it would break.

I built models, compared internal data to public filings, found the gaps, and documented everything.

James worked beside me. "You're fast at this."

"I used to do it professionally."

"McKinsey?"

I froze. How did he know? He must have seen my face.

"Keller told the senior team. Said you worked at McKinsey. That you understand corporate analysis better than anyone."

"I wasn't there long."

"Long enough to know how to spot fraud."

I didn't answer; I kept working. By 2 PM, I had it: a complete analysis showing the gap between reported and actual subscribers. Eight quarters of fraud, growing worse each quarter. Tyler had lied to investors repeatedly, knowingly, deliberately. This would destroy him.

I pulled up my phone. Time for Grace's call. FaceTime connected, and Linda's face appeared.

"Hi, Mom."

"Hi." Her voice was gentle, tired.

"Can I talk to Grace?"

"She's at school." Of course she was. 2 PM. Grace wouldn't be home until 3:30 PM.

"I forgot the schedule."

"I figured you would. First day back at work. Your head's probably spinning."

The understanding in her voice surprised me.

"How is she?" I asked.

Linda sighed. "This morning was hard. She cried when she woke up and you weren't here. Kept asking when you were coming home."

My chest tightened. "What did you tell her?"

"The truth: twenty-eight more days, four more weeks. Then you come home with information about Uncle Leo." Linda paused. "She asked if the bad people would go to time-out."

"What did you say?"

"I said yes, that grown-up timeout is called consequences, and that Mama's working to make sure they face consequences." Linda's voice got softer. "She seemed to understand that better: the idea that you're catching bad people, making them face consequences for hurting Uncle Leo."

I closed my eyes, relief flooding through me.

"She still cried," Linda continued, "but it wasn't the same kind of crying. It was sad crying, not angry crying. She understands you're doing something important. She just wishes you could do it here."

"Me too."

"But this is about Leo." Linda's voice became firm. "And after seven years of not knowing, of never getting justice... if this one month gives us answers about who killed my son, then it's worth it. Grace will be okay. I'll make sure of that."

The words hit me hard. Linda supporting me. Linda choosing to believe in this.

"Thank you," I whispered.

"Don't thank me yet. Just keep your promise. One month. Twenty-eight days. Then you come home with the evidence, and you don't leave again."

"I won't."

"I'm holding you to that." But her voice wasn't cold; it was just honest. "Call at 4:30 when she's home from school. And Olivia? I put the calendar on the fridge. Grace and I are crossing off each day together so she can see the number getting smaller."

"That's a good idea."

"It was her idea, actually. She wanted to count down. Like counting down to Christmas."

My throat was tight. "She's so smart."

"She's your daughter. Of course she is."

Linda hung up.

When I came back, Marcus was waiting.

"Got a minute?"

"Sure."

He pulled up a document. "The whistleblower sent another message an hour ago."

My stomach tightened. "What does it say?"

"They're offering more: board meeting minutes, strategic planning documents, and Tyler's personal emails with Margaret about covering up losses."

"They're giving us everything."

Marcus nodded. "Which is great. But also strange. Why risk so much? Why expose themselves like this?"

"Maybe they have immunity. Maybe they cut a deal with the SEC."

"Maybe. Or maybe they have another reason."

"Like what?"

Marcus looked at me. "Like they want Tyler gone so badly they're willing to commit career suicide to make it happen."

"That's what a whistleblower does."

"Yeah. But usually they want something in return: protection, money, recognition."

"This person wants none of that. This person is completely anonymous. This person is not asking for anything."

"He or she is just asking us to destroy Tyler."

Marcus pulled up the original email again and read it out loud. *I've watched Tyler Carrington destroy this company for three years.*

He paused and looked at me. "This isn't someone protecting the company. This is someone who hates Tyler personally."

"Does it matter?"

"It matters if they're feeding us information that's true but misleading. It matters if they have their own agenda."

I thought about Margaret, about how she'd manipulated the media, planted stories, controlled narratives.

What if this whistleblower was doing the same thing?

"What does Keller think?"

"Keller thinks Tyler's guilty regardless. Whether the whistleblower is pure or not, the fraud is real. The emails are real. The internal data matches what we suspected."

"So we use it."

"We use it. But carefully."

Marcus left me alone with the documents. I spent the next three hours verifying everything, making sure the numbers aligned, that the patterns made sense, and that this wasn't a trap. It all checked out. Tyler was guilty. The fraud was real. By 7 PM, I had a report. Twenty-three pages. Detailed. Damning. I sent it to Keller and Miranda.

Miranda's response came in five minutes: *This is perfect. Exactly what we needed. Take tomorrow morning off. You've earned it.* But I didn't want a morning off. I wanted to keep working. Because working meant I wasn't thinking about Grace. I wasn't thinking about the choice I'd made. I wasn't thinking about twenty-seven more days.

My phone buzzed. Email from Keller.

Excellent work today. The fraud case is solid. Tomorrow we start building the coalition. BlackRock meeting at 2 PM. They control twenty percent of CMG. If we get them, we've won.

I need you there. Your analysis. Your presentation of the fraud evidence. They need to hear it from you.

Tomorrow. One day into a month-long war. And I was already getting pulled deeper. I texted Miranda: *I'll be there.*

Her response: *Good. This is how we win.*

I put my phone down and stared at the ceiling. This is how we win. Tyler's destruction. Leo's justice. Answers for Linda. And Grace waiting at home with a calendar on the fridge.

I closed my eyes, but I couldn't sleep. Somewhere in the darkness, I heard Leo's voice. Not a hallucination. Not a ghost. Just a memory.

You were always the smart one, Livvy. The one who knew how to plan. But Dad was smart too. And his plans destroyed us. Be careful you don't do the same thing.

I opened my eyes and stared into the darkness. Leo was right. Dad had been smart. He'd planned. He'd promised. He'd told himself, "just one more." And look what happened. But I wasn't Dad. I had Linda's support. I had Grace's understanding. I had a calendar counting down to the day I'd come home. Twenty-seven more days. That's all. And then I'd keep my promise. I had to.

The next morning, I woke up at 5 AM to a text. Anonymous number.

You're wasting your time with Tyler. He's small. Margaret is the real enemy. And she's watching you.

My blood went cold. Who had this number? Who knew I was working with Keller? I sat on the bed, holding my phone and staring at the message.

Margaret is watching you. The words sent ice through my chest because I knew they were true. Margaret always watched. Always knew. Always struck when you least expected it. And I'd just walked into a battle with her, thinking I was invisible. Thinking I was safe. But Margaret Carrington didn't lose. And she'd already beaten me once before. What made me think this time would be different?

Chapter Six

When Grace Stopped Breathing

THE PHONE RANG AT 2:47 AM. I was still awake, staring at my laptop. Numbers blurred together: subscriber data, revenue projections, the case that would destroy Tyler. The BlackRock presentation was open on my screen. Final version. Ready for this afternoon.

Linda's name lit up the screen. My stomach knew before my brain did. It dropped like a stone. I couldn't make my thumb move to answer. Couldn't breathe. Because Linda never called at 2:47 AM unless something was wrong. I answered.

"Hello?"

"Olivia."

That's all she said. Just my name. But her voice trembled around it, shaking, crying. My chest went tight.

"What happened?"

"Grace had a seizure." The words came out like she was choking. "We're in the ER. They're running tests."

The room tilted. The laptop slid off my knees and hit the floor. I didn't hear it. Grace. Seizure. ER. Those were the only words that existed.

"What happened?" My voice didn't sound like mine. Too high. Too thin.

"High fever. She was sleeping. I checked on her around midnight, and she was fine. Just hot. I gave her medicine. Then at two, I heard this sound." Linda's breath caught and shuddered. "This awful sound. Like she couldn't breathe. And when I got to her room, she was—" She couldn't finish. Just made this horrible choking sound.

"She was convulsing. Her whole body. I called 911. They came so fast, but it felt like forever. She stopped breathing for a second. Olivia, she stopped breathing."

I was moving. Didn't remember standing up or grabbing my bag. Just moving, throwing things in: laptop, clothes, phone charger. My hands shook so badly I couldn't zip the bag. I kept missing. Kept trying. Kept missing. "I'm coming. Right now. I'm getting on the next flight."

"They have her stable." Linda's voice cracked on the word "stable," like it was a lie she was trying to believe. "The fever's coming down. They said it was probably a febrile seizure. Common in kids with FASD. But they're running tests to make sure."

I finally got the zipper closed, grabbed my coat, my phone, my keys. My phone buzzed. Text from Miranda. *Final run-through 9 AM. BlackRock at 2 PM. This is it.*

The meeting. Today. In eleven hours. If I got on a plane right now, I'd miss it. Miss everything.

"I'll be there in four hours," I said to Linda. "Maybe less. Tell her I'm coming."

"Olivia." Linda's voice became quiet, different. "She asked for you."

The words stopped me right there in the middle of the hotel room, coat half on, bag in one hand.

"What?"

"When she woke up in the ambulance, the first thing she said was, 'Where's Mama?' She seemed to forget that you were in NY. And I had to tell her again." Linda's voice grew gentle, understanding. "I had to remind her you were in New York, working to catch the bad people. And you know what she said?"

I couldn't speak.

"She said, 'Mama being brave.' Like she understood. Like she was proud of you."

My throat closed completely.

"The doctors say she's stable," Linda continued, softer now. "The fever's breaking. She's sleeping. I'm with her. And honestly, Olivia? I think you should stay there. Finish what you're doing. Because if you come home now, you'll just be here worrying about what you're missing. And that won't help Grace."

"But she needs me—"

"She needs you healthy and whole and not torn apart by regret," Linda said firmly. "She needs you to finish this work so you can come home and actually be present with her. Not half here, half wishing you were somewhere else."

"Mom, she stopped breathing—"

"And now she's breathing fine. The fever's almost gone. The doctors aren't worried. I'm with her every second." Linda's voice softened. "You can FaceTime her when she wakes up. You can talk to her. And then you can finish what you went there to do. For Leo."

I stood there, coat half on, bag in hand. The meeting was in eleven hours. Everything I'd worked for. Everything I'd sacrificed Grace for. And Grace was in the hospital, asking for me.

"Are you sure?" My voice broke.

"I'm sure. She's safe. I promise you. She's safe." Linda paused. "But Olivia? After you're done there, after you finish this, you come home and you stay home. You understand? Grace needs you. Not just for emergencies, but for normal days, boring nights, and all the small moments you've been missing."

"I understand."

"Good. Now I'm going to hang up so you can get ready for whatever you're doing today. I'll text you updates every hour. You call Grace when she wakes up. And you finish strong. Okay?"

"Okay."

"I love you. And so does Grace. Even when you're not here."

She hung up. I sat on the bed, put my bag down, and took my coat off.

Grace was stable. Linda was with her. The doctors said febrile seizures were common in kids with FASD. She was safe. But my hands were still shaking. My chest was still tight.

I opened my laptop and looked at flight times to Cleveland. There was a 6 AM. I could make it if I left right now. Be there by 10 AM. Miss the 9 AM run-through. Miss the 2 PM BlackRock meeting. Miss everything. Or I could stay. Trust Linda. Trust the doctors. Trust that Grace would forgive me.

My finger hovered over the search bar. Grace's face filled my mind. In that ambulance. Asking for Mama. Then the presentation on my screen. Tyler's fraud. Margaret's crimes. Leo's justice. I closed the flight search and opened the presentation instead. I'd stay. I'd go to the meeting. I'd do what I came here to do. And I'd hate myself for it. But I'd do it anyway.

My phone buzzed. Text from Linda. *Fever down to 99.8. She's sleeping peacefully. The doctor says she can go home in the morning.*

Relief flooded through me. Then another text. *You're doing the right thing. Whatever you're working on there, it matters. Leo would be proud. Grace will understand when she's older. I love you.*

I texted back: *Love you too. Thank you for being there for her. Always. Now get some rest. Big day today.*

She didn't even know what today was. She didn't know about BlackRock. She didn't know this was the moment everything had been building toward. She just trusted me. She believed I was doing something that mattered.

My phone rang. Different number. Richard. My banker. I answered, "Hello?"

"Olivia. I hope I'm not calling too late. I heard about Grace."

My stomach dropped. "How did you—"

"Linda called me this afternoon. She asked if I knew any pediatric specialists in Cleveland. I made some calls and got her connected to the best FASD team at Cleveland Clinic."

"You did that?"

"Of course." His voice was gentle. "I know we haven't spoken since the margin call crisis, but I've been following the stock and watching what you're doing. I wanted you to know that what you're attempting with Carrington Media, going up against Margaret like this, it's incredibly brave. Also incredibly dangerous."

"I know."

"Do you?" He paused. "Olivia, Margaret Carrington doesn't lose. Not ever. She has resources you can't imagine. Her head of security is a former Mossad agent named Yael

Rothstein. The woman ran counterintelligence operations for fifteen years. If Margaret wants to know where you are, what you're doing, or who you're talking to, Yael finds out. Always."

My blood went cold. "Why are you telling me this?"

"Because you need to know what you're up against. Margaret doesn't just have money. She has intelligence capabilities that rival small governments. And right now, she's using all of it to destroy you."

"How do you know this?"

"I have clients who've gone up against her before. They've lost everything. One even had to leave the country." He took a breath. "I'm calling because I want you to be careful. And I want you to know that if you need anything, like financial advice, connections, or just someone to talk to, I'm here."

"Thank you," I whispered. He hung up.

I sat there, my heart pounding. Mossad. Former counterintelligence. That's how Margaret always knew. That's how she knew about Grace. My phone buzzed. Unknown number.

Your daughter is sick in the hospital. I bet you're debating whether to go or stay right now. Let me make a prediction: You'll choose revenge over your daughter. Just like your father chose alcohol over his family. You're exactly what you swore you'd never become.

My blood went cold. I stared at the message. I read it again. And again. This wasn't just tracking. This was psychological warfare. Someone knew exactly where to cut to make it hurt most. I called Miranda immediately.

"Someone just texted me. Anonymous. They know about Grace. They know I'm deciding whether to stay or go."

"What did it say?"

I read it to her. Silence on the other end.

"Miranda?"

"Send me a screenshot. I'll have our security team trace it."

"Richard just called. He told me about Margaret's head of security, Yael Rothstein. Former Mossad."

More silence.

"He's right," Miranda said finally. "We knew Margaret had serious security, but we didn't know exactly who. If it's Yael Rothstein, that explains everything: the tracking, the surveillance, how she always seems to know our moves before we make them."

"So what do we do?"

"We assume everything is compromised. Every call, every text, every location. We assume she knows." Miranda's voice was grim. "But we proceed anyway. Because stopping now means she wins."

"This is the second anonymous message," I said. "Yesterday someone warned me that Margaret was watching. That Tyler was small and she was the real enemy."

"You didn't tell me about that one."

"I forgot. Everything with Grace—"

"Don't forget things like that again. Send me both screenshots. Now."

She hung up. I sat there, heart pounding. Margaret had a former Mossad agent tracking me, watching me, predicting my every move. My phone buzzed again. Linda.

She's asking for you. Can you FaceTime?

I hit the call button immediately. Linda's face appeared. Then Grace's. She looked small, tired, her hospital gown too big on her little body.

"Mama!"

"Hi, baby. I heard you weren't feeling good."

"Was sick." Her voice was hoarse, small. "But better now."

"That's good. I'm so glad you're feeling better."

"Gamma says you're coming home soon?"

I looked at Linda's face and saw the warning there. Don't lie. Don't make promises you won't keep.

"Not yet, baby. Mama still has work. But soon."

Grace's face fell. "How soon?"

"Twenty-six more sleeps. Then Mama comes home and stays home."

"That's a lot." Her eyes filled with tears. "That's so many."

"I know, sweetheart. I know it feels like a lot. But Mama's doing something important. For Uncle Leo. Remember?"

"Uncle Leo in heaven."

"That's right. And Mama's trying to catch the bad people who hurt him. So they get in trouble."

"Big trouble?"

"Really big trouble."

Grace nodded, processing. Then: "Okay. But Mama? After you catch them, you come home?"

"Yes. I promise."

She held up her hand to the screen, little fingers spread wide. "Love you."

I pressed my hand against the screen, matching hers. "Love you too, baby. So much."

Linda's voice: "Say goodnight to Mama, Grace. You need rest."

"Night, Mama."

"Goodnight, sweetheart."

The screen went black. I sat there, staring at nothing. Grace in a hospital bed, asking when I was coming home. And me choosing revenge over her hospital bedside.

The knock on my door came at 10:23 AM. I'd been awake since six. FaceTimed Grace at seven. She was being discharged, going home with Linda. Everything was fine. So why did the knock sound wrong? Too soft, too deliberate. I opened the door.

Margaret Carrington stood in the hallway. Perfect black suit. Cold eyes. But something was different now. Something that looked like barely contained rage.

"Hello, Olivia."

My heart forgot how to beat.

"How did you—"

"Get your room number?" She walked past me into the room. Didn't wait for permission. "I know a lot of things. Did you really think you could stay here without me knowing?"

She turned, looking at me like I was something she'd found on the bottom of her shoe.

"My people know where you are every minute of every day. They know who you talk to. They know what you're planning."

Margaret walked to my laptop and glanced at the screen, at the presentation slides, Tyler's emails, the fraud evidence.

"BlackRock meeting at 2 PM. Very important meeting. You think you're going to convince them to vote against us."

She turned to face me, and now I could see it: the fury beneath her perfect exterior.

"You acquired ten percent of my company." The words came out sharp and cutting. "You. An alcoholic prostitute who couldn't hold a job at Nordstrom. You borrowed money to buy ten percent of the company I spent thirty years building."

She stepped closer. I wanted to back away, but I made myself stand still.

"How dare you. How dare you think you have any right to challenge me, to come after my family, to try to destroy what I built."

"Tyler destroyed it himself—"

"Tyler made mistakes!" Her voice rose, actually rising. The first crack in her perfect control. "Every CEO makes mistakes. But you don't get to use those mistakes to steal my company."

"I'm not stealing anything. I'm exposing fraud—"

"You're seeking revenge." She cut through my words. "Because I wouldn't let you destroy Tyler. So now you're trying to destroy us both."

The words hung in the air, raw and true.

"But you know what?" Margaret's voice got quiet again, calm, which somehow felt more dangerous. "You won't be able to do anything with that ten percent. You think buying shares makes you powerful? You think it gives you control?"

She laughed, actually laughed.

"Here's what you don't understand," Margaret said quietly. "I've been destroying people longer than you've been alive, and I'm very, very good at it. I've been fighting off activists and hostile takeovers for three decades. You're not the first person to try to take my company. You won't be the last. And you'll fail just like all the others."

She pulled out her phone and showed me photos. Grace in the hospital bed last night, wires and tubes. Linda crying in the waiting room. The ambulance pulling up to the ER.

"I have people at every hospital in Cleveland, every school, every therapy center Grace attends. I know where your daughter is every single minute."

My blood turned to ice.

"I could make one phone call," Margaret said softly. "And Child Protective Services would show up at Linda's door. An anonymous tip about an unstable mother who abandons her sick child to pursue revenge. Who has a history of prostitution, alcoholism, and mental health crises."

"You wouldn't—"

"I would. I've done worse. Ask the last person who tried to take my company. He lost everything: his business, his reputation, his family." She smiled. Cold. Sharp. "He lives in Singapore now. Couldn't show his face in the U.S. after what I did to him."

She put her phone away. "But I'm not here to threaten you. I'm here to offer you one last chance."

She walked to the window and looked out at the city. "If you back off now, if you don't attend the BlackRock meeting, if you sell your shares and go back to Ohio and never speak my family's name again, then I will forgive what you've done so far."

She turned. "I'll let you keep your small YouTube business, your reputation. I'll even let you keep you and your family safe."

My hands started shaking.

"But if you attend that meeting today, if you continue this war against my family, then I will destroy you. Not quickly. Not mercifully. Slowly. Piece by piece. Until there's nothing left."

She stepped closer. "I will take everything: your business. I'll make sure every mother in your network knows you abandoned your sick daughter. They'll leave you. Your daughter. I'll leak her medical records. Show the world she has FASD. Ruin any chance she has at a normal life."

My chest was so tight I couldn't breathe.

"And when you're broke, desperate, and alone, when everyone you love has been destroyed, I'll make sure you know it was all your fault. That you could have prevented it. That you chose this."

She walked to the door and turned. "I've given you one opportunity to walk away. Don't waste it."

She left. I stood there, alone, shaking so hard I had to sit down. Margaret wasn't bluffing. She had former Mossad tracking me. She had photos of Grace in the hospital. She had the power to destroy everything. And I'd just been given one last chance to walk away.

My phone buzzed. Miranda.

Car will be there at 1:30. Don't be late.

I stared at the text. The meeting was in three and a half hours. I could walk away. Go home to Grace. Keep her safe. Keep Linda safe. Keep everything I'd built. Or I could go to that meeting. Risk everything. Fight Margaret and probably lose. Grace's face filled my mind. In that hospital bed. Asking when I was coming home. Then Leo's face. Beaten. Alone. No one ever held accountable. I picked up my phone.

I texted Miranda back: *I'll be ready.*

Then, I opened my laptop and looked at the presentation one more time. Margaret thought she'd scared me into backing down. She was wrong. I was going to that meeting, and I was going to fight, even if it cost me everything.

Chapter Seven

BlackRock

I ARRIVED AT BLACKROCK at 1:45 PM. Fifteen minutes early. Plenty of time. Keller and Miranda were waiting in the lobby, both tense but ready.

"Ready?" Keller asked.

"Ready."

"Let's go to the conference room," Miranda said. "Four portfolio managers. They control 20% of Carrington's stock. If we convince them, Tyler's finished."

We walked down the hallway. My heart was pounding, but my mind was clear. I'd done this a hundred times at McKinsey. I walked into rooms full of skeptical executives and won them over with data. This was no different. We'd prepared for weeks. We had the evidence, the facts, and the truth. Margaret could make all the threats she wanted, but she couldn't change the numbers, couldn't change Tyler's emails, couldn't change reality.

Keller opened the conference room door. We walked in and froze.

Margaret Carrington sat at the head of the table. Perfect posture. Perfect suit. Perfect smile. Surrounded by the four BlackRock portfolio managers, laughing at something she'd just said. My breath stopped.

No, no, no. She looked up as we entered. Her smile got wider, but her eyes were cold and triumphant.

"David. Miranda. Ms. Parker. Thank you for joining us. I was just telling our friends from BlackRock about some exciting changes at Carrington Media."

Keller's face went white. "What is she doing here?"

The lead BlackRock manager stood. "Mrs. Carrington arrived about thirty minutes ago. She expressed a desire to address the concerns directly. We felt it was appropriate to hear from both sides."

"Both sides?" Miranda's voice was sharp. "This was supposed to be our presentation—"

"And it still is," the manager said calmly. "But Mrs. Carrington has relevant information. We'd like to hear everything before making a decision."

Keller looked at me, his face asking the question: Can you do this with her in the room?

I nodded and forced myself to breathe. I could do this. I'd presented to tougher audiences, more hostile rooms. Margaret was just another executive trying to protect a failing company.

We sat down. I pulled out my laptop and connected to the screen. My hands were steady, my mind clear. McKinsey training kicked in: block out distractions, focus on the data, and deliver the story.

"Shall we begin?" The BlackRock manager's voice was neutral.

I stood and walked to the front of the room. Margaret watched, her face calm, almost pleasant. I pulled up the first slide.

"Carrington Media has been lying to investors for three years." My voice was strong and clear. "They've inflated subscriber numbers, manipulated revenue recognition, and misrepresented the health of their core business. Today, I'm going to show you exactly how they did it." I pulled up the subscriber data. Clean. Precise. The numbers I'd verified a dozen times.

"In Q2 2024, Carrington reported 3.2 million sub-scribers. But internal data shows the actual number was 2.7 million. A gap of 500,000 fake accounts."

I clicked to the next slide: the churn analysis. They hid this by not counting canceled subscriptions for 90 days. Subscribers would cancel, but Carrington kept them on the books for another three months. When investors saw the numbers, they looked healthy. But underneath, the business was bleeding users.

The BlackRock managers were nodding, taking notes, following along. Good. This was working. I pulled up Tyler's email.

"This email from Tyler Carrington to his CFO shows intent. He wrote, 'I don't care about the actual churn rate. I care what the Street sees.' That's securities fraud. Deliberate misrepresentation of material facts."

"May I ask a question?" Margaret's voice was soft and polite.

I stopped and looked at her.

"Of course," the lead manager said.

Margaret stood, walked toward the front of the room, and stopped a few feet away from me. Close enough that I could see her face clearly, see the calculation in her eyes.

"Ms. Parker, your analysis is very thorough. Very impressive. McKinsey taught you well."

The words were compliments, but her tone was something else. Something that made my skin crawl.

"Thank you," I said carefully.

"I'm curious, though. You left McKinsey five years ago, correct?"

"Yes."

"Under difficult circumstances, if I recall." Her voice was gentle and sympathetic. "There was an incident at a Peninsula Hotel event. Very public. Very embarrassing. The video went viral."

My chest tightened, but I kept my face neutral.

"I had a personal crisis. I've since recovered and built a successful business."

"Of course. Of course." Margaret smiled. "I admire your resilience. It takes strength to come back from something like that, especially when there were addiction issues involved."

The room temperature dropped. I could feel the Black-Rock managers shifting, uncomfortable.

"My past struggles don't affect the accuracy of my analysis," I said firmly. "The data speaks for itself."

"Absolutely. I agree completely." Margaret turned to the managers. "Ms. Parker's data is accurate. Tyler did send that email. The subscriber numbers were inflated. All of it is true."

Wait. What? She was agreeing with me?

"However," Margaret continued, "what Ms. Parker may not know is that I've been aware of these issues for six months." She walked to the screen and pulled out her own laptop. "May I?"

The lead manager nodded. My presentation disappeared; hers replaced it. Documents appeared on screen: official audit reports, board minutes, SEC filings.

"In September, I commissioned an independent audit. The audit confirmed everything Ms. Parker found." Margaret's voice was calm and professional. "In October, I placed Tyler on administrative leave. In November, I hired a new CFO to clean up our financial reporting." She looked at the BlackRock managers.

"And two weeks ago, the board voted unanimously to remove Tyler as CEO. Permanently. I'm taking over as interim CEO while we search for his replacement."

No. No, this wasn't possible. She'd fired Tyler. Already fired him. Before we could.

"We're filing amended financial statements within thirty days," Margaret continued. "Complete transparency with the SEC. Taking full responsibility for the errors."

She turned to me. Her smile was kind. Almost motherly. "Ms. Parker, I want to thank you. Your analysis helped confirm what our auditors found. But I'm afraid you're a few months behind. I already fixed the problem."

My mind was racing, trying to find the angle, the weakness.

"You knew about the fraud for six months," I said, my voice sharp. "But you didn't disclose it to investors. That's a violation of securities law. You had a duty to report—"

"We disclosed the audit in our 10-Q filing," Margaret interrupted smoothly. "It's public record. Perhaps you missed it."

She pulled up the filing on screen. There it was, buried in footnote 47. Technically disclosed. Technically legal.

"You buried it," I said.

"We disclosed it appropriately per SEC guidelines," Margaret corrected. "There's a difference."

She looked at the BlackRock managers. "Tyler is out. The fraud is being corrected. The company is being restructured. Everything Ms. Parker wanted to accomplish, I've already done. The only question is whether you want to support my turnaround plan or waste six months in a costly proxy fight."

The lead manager spoke. "Mrs. Carrington, this is unexpected. But it does change the calculus."

"I understand." Margaret pulled up financial projections. "Without Tyler's failed acquisitions and with proper accounting, we're actually quite profitable. Strong content library. Loyal subscriber base. Significant growth potential."

She was good. Really good. Taking my entire case and making it hers. I had to break through. I had to find something that would shake them.

"You're forgetting about the criminal operations," I said. "Your nightclub in Millfield. Club Vertical. Money laundering. Gang payments. That's not Tyler's fraud. That's yours."

The room went very quiet. Margaret's face didn't change. Didn't even flicker.

"I'm not sure what you're referring to," she said calmly.

"Club Vertical. You opened it in 2015. You used it to launder money for organized crime. The same gangs that—" My voice caught. "The same gangs that killed my brother."

There. I'd said it. The real reason. The thing that mattered. Margaret's eyes softened. Sympathetic. Understanding.

"I'm so sorry about your brother, Ms. Parker. Truly. I know he died in 2014 in Millfield. Gang violence is a terrible tragedy."

She turned to the BlackRock managers. "I don't know what Ms. Parker is alleging about my businesses. But I do know that she has very personal reasons for wanting to hurt my family. Her brother died tragically. Tyler had a relationship with her that ended badly. And now she's here, making accusations without evidence."

"I have evidence—"

"Do you?" Margaret's voice was still gentle. But there was steel underneath. "Because if you had evidence of criminal activity, you'd go to the FBI, not to BlackRock."

She stepped closer to me, close enough to whisper. But her voice carried. Everyone heard.

"Ms. Parker, I understand what you're going through. I really do. You lost your brother. You've struggled with addiction. You had a traumatic experience with my son. And now you're trying to make sense of it all by creating this narrative where I'm the villain."

She looked at me with something that looked almost like pity. "But revenge isn't justice. And accusations aren't evidence. If you have proof of criminal activity, show it. Otherwise, you're just hurting yourself. And your daughter."

My daughter. The words hit like ice water. She'd brought up Grace. In front of everyone. Subtle. Coded. But unmistakable. "My daughter has nothing to do with this," I said, my voice shaking now.

"Of course not," Margaret said quickly. "I only meant you have a young child at home. Three years old, correct? With special needs? It must be so hard being away from her, especially when she's sick."

My hands started shaking.

"I just think," Margaret continued softly, "that maybe you should focus on taking care of your daughter instead of pursuing this vendetta. She needs her mother, especially with her medical issues."

The room was spinning. I couldn't breathe. She was doing this on purpose. Bringing up Grace. Bringing up the hospital. Reminding me that she had power over my daughter.

"I—" My voice came out broken. "I'm fighting for justice."

"I know you believe that," Margaret said, her voice still kind, still understanding. "But look at where this fight has brought you. Away from your daughter. Making accusations you can't prove. Reliving trauma instead of healing from it."

She turned to the BlackRock managers. "Ms. Parker is brilliant. Her analysis is thorough. But she's also deeply wounded. And wounded people don't always see clearly."

She looked back at me. "I hope you get the help you need, Olivia. I really do. And I hope you go home to your daughter and focus on what really matters."

The words were gentle, caring. But I heard the threat underneath. Go home. Leave this alone. Or I'll destroy Grace too.

"Ms. Parker, did you want to add anything?" The lead manager's voice was distant, already decided.

I stood there, shaking, unable to speak. Because Margaret had just done what I couldn't defend against. She hadn't fought my data. She'd fought me. Painted me as traumatized, obsessed, unstable. And worst of all, she'd threatened Grace in front of everyone without anyone else even hearing the threat.

I looked at Keller. His face was gray. He'd seen it too. Seen me crumble. I looked at Miranda. She was staring at the table. I looked at Margaret. She smiled, patient, victorious.

"I don't have anything to add," I whispered.

"Then I think we're done here," the lead manager said. "Mrs. Carrington, thank you for your transparency."

Margaret nodded, shook hands with each of them, then walked past me to the door. She leaned in as she passed, whispered so only I could hear.

"Next time you choose a meeting over your sick daughter, make sure you win."

She left. The BlackRock managers stood, shook Keller's hand perfunctorily, and avoided my eyes. Then they left too. The door closed. Silence.

Keller's phone buzzed. He looked at it. His face went expressionless. "They're staying with Margaret."

The words echoed in the empty room.

"What?" Miranda's voice was barely a whisper.

"BlackRock just emailed. They're declining our proposal. Supporting Margaret as interim CEO."

He looked at me. His eyes were cold. Disappointed. "We lost."

I stood there at the front of the room, my presentation abandoned. We hadn't lost because my analysis was wrong. We'd lost because Margaret had turned my trauma into a weapon, used Grace against me, and made me look unstable. And I'd let her.

"I'm sorry," I whispered. "I'm so sorry."

"It's done," Keller said, his voice flat. Dead. "We're done."

He walked out. Miranda followed. I stood alone in the conference room. Margaret hadn't beaten my case. She'd beaten me. And she'd done it by threatening the only thing that mattered. My daughter.

I flew home that night. Sat on the plane in the dark, staring at nothing. We'd lost. Not because my analysis was wrong. Not because the data wasn't there. Not because I wasn't good enough. We'd lost because Margaret had turned my trauma into a weapon, used Grace against me, and made me look unstable in front of everyone.

Tyler was fired, but not because of me. Because Margaret did it first. The fraud was being fixed, but not because I exposed it. Because Margaret exposed it herself. And worst of all, she'd threatened Grace.

"Your daughter... three years old... with special needs... especially when she's sick."

She'd known about last night. Known Grace was in the hospital. Known I'd chosen the meeting over my daughter's bedside. And she'd used it to destroy me.

I landed in Cleveland at 11:34 PM. Drove to Linda's house. The lights were off. Everyone was asleep. I sat in the car, staring at the dark house. My phone buzzed. Linda.

Heard the car. Come inside. Grace is sleeping, but you need to see her.

I got out and walked to the door. Linda opened it before I could knock. Her face was gentle but knowing.

"You lost." Not a question. A statement.

"How did you know?"

"Because you look like someone who just lost everything." She stepped aside. "What happened?"

"Margaret was there. At the meeting. She'd already fired Tyler. Already fixed the fraud. She made me look obsessed, traumatized. And then she..." I couldn't finish.

"She what?"

"She brought up Grace. In front of everyone. Talked about her being sick last night. Made it sound concerned. But it was a threat."

Linda's face went hard. "She threatened Grace?"

"Not directly. Never directly. But I heard it. 'I hope you go home to your daughter and focus on what really matters.' Like she was giving me permission to leave. But really telling me what she'd do if I didn't."

Linda was quiet for a long moment. Then: "Grace cried for an hour tonight, asking when you were coming home, asking if you still loved her."

The words cut through me. "Of course I still love her."

Linda touched my arm. "Go see her. Then we need to talk. You need to decide if you're coming home or if you're staying to fight Margaret."

"How can I keep fighting? She just used Grace against me. What happens next time? What happens if I actually get close to winning?"

"Did you get the evidence about Leo? About Margaret's clubs? About the gangs?"

I shook my head. "No, I don't have the evidence from Kel ler... We just lost. Should I keep fighting?"

"That's up to you. I can't tell you what's right. I want justice for Leo. But I also want Grace safe. And I don't know if you can have both."

She walked away, leaving me standing in the hallway. I walked to Grace's room and opened the door quietly. She was sleeping, face peaceful, thumb in her mouth. I sat on the edge of her bed, watching her breathe.

Margaret had turned her into a weapon, into leverage, into the thing that would make me stop. And it was working. Grace stirred, turned toward me, and opened her eyes.

"Mama?"

"Hi, baby. I'm here."

"You came." Her voice was small, surprised, like she hadn't expected me to keep this promise either.

"I came." She reached for me. I lay down next to her and held her.

"Love you, Mama."

"I love you too, sweetheart. So, so much."

"You done catching bad people?"

The question hit hard. "I don't know, baby. It's harder than I thought."

"You catch them today?"

"No. I lost today."

She was quiet, processing. Then: "That's okay. Try again?" The simple wisdom of a three-year-old. No complicated analysis. Just try again.

"I don't know... I don't know."

She curled against me, already falling back asleep. Safe. Trusting. I didn't know if I could walk away. I didn't know if I could fight again. She fell asleep in my arms. I lay there, holding my daughter, staring at the dark ceiling.

Margaret had beaten me today. Not with better data. Not with superior strategy. With psychological warfare. With threats against Grace. And she'd do it again, every time I got close, every time I threatened her. Could I keep fighting knowing that?

My phone buzzed. Unknown number.

You lost today. Margaret won by using your daughter against you. She'll do it again if you keep fighting. Go home, Olivia. Grace needs you more than Leo needs justice. Some battles aren't worth winning.

I stared at the message. This was different. Every other message had pushed me to fight, to stay, to finish what I started. But now they were telling me to stop. Who was this person? Why had they changed their mind? But maybe they were right. Maybe Margaret had shown me exactly what would happen if I kept fighting. She'd use Grace over and over until there was nothing left.

I set the phone down and looked at Grace sleeping in my arms. Twenty-six more days. That's what I'd promised. But what if I just stopped? What if I stayed home tomorrow and never went back? Margaret would win. Tyler would face some consequences, but not enough. Leo's killers would stay free. The gangs Margaret funded would keep operating. But Grace would have her mother. Safe. Present. Not choosing revenge over her anymore.

I reached for my bag and pulled out Grandpa's compass. The brass was cold in my palm. Heavy. The glass face still cracked from when Dad dropped it years ago, the crack running north to south, splitting the directions. Dad had given this to me when I was eight. He told me I was his compass, that I always knew what was right.

"This compass will find you the right path," he'd said. Dad's compass had been broken for years, the crack spreading slowly. I held the compass up and watched the needle spin in the dim light from the hallway. Back and forth. Back and forth. And now I was lost, following a broken compass toward revenge instead of home.

The needle settled, pointing north through the crack. North wasn't Margaret. North wasn't Tyler. North wasn't justice for Leo. North was Grace, asleep in my arms, trusting me one more time. I closed my fingers around the compass, feeling the crack against my palm. Maybe the compass wasn't broken. Maybe north had been there all along. I just kept looking in the wrong direction.

Chapter Eight

Waiting to Be Fired

I SPENT THREE DAYS at Linda's house after the Black-Rock disaster. Three days trying to be present with Grace. Three days helping with meals and bedtime and the small routines I'd missed. Three days sitting at the kitchen table, expecting the world to end. But nothing came.

No email from Keller firing me. No call from Miranda telling me I'd destroyed everything. No threatening message from Margaret saying she'd won. Just silence. And somehow, the silence was worse than screaming would have been.

On the fourth morning, Grace woke up happy, babbling in her crib. Normal sounds. Safe sounds. I went to her room and found her standing up, holding her stuffed bear, her face lighting up when she saw me.

"Mama!"

"Hi, baby. Good morning."

"Up! Up!" I lifted her out and held her against my chest. She wrapped her arms around my neck and squeezed tight.

"Hungry," she said into my shoulder.

"Let's get you breakfast."

Linda was already in the kitchen, making eggs. She looked up when we came in. Her face was gentle but knowing.

"How'd you sleep?" she asked.

"Not great."

"Me neither." She set a plate down for Grace and cut the eggs into tiny pieces. "You keep checking your phone."

"Waiting for Keller to fire me."

"Has he called?"

"No. That's what's making me nervous."

Linda poured coffee and slid a mug across the table to me. "Maybe he's not firing you."

"I lost the most important meeting. Margaret destroyed me."

"She used Grace against you. That's different." Linda's voice was firm. "That wasn't your failure. That was her being ruthless."

"Either way, we lost."

"Did you?" Linda sat down.

"Tyler's out. The fraud is being fixed. Margaret exposed everything. She beat me to it."

Linda was quiet for a moment, watching Grace eat. Then: "You know what I keep thinking about?"

"What?"

"That night in the hospital when Grace stopped breathing." Linda's voice grew softer. "You chose to stay for the meeting. And I told you it was okay. That it mattered."

"Mom—"

"Let me finish." She looked at me. "I've been wondering if I was wrong. Whether I should have told you to come home. Whether Leo's justice is worth Grace's pain."

My throat tightened.

"And I don't know the answer," Linda said. "But I know this: You came home. You've been here for three days. Present. Playing with her. Being her mother."

"Because I lost. There's nothing left to fight for."

"Is that true?" Linda tilted her head. "Or is that what you're telling yourself so you don't have to decide?"

Grace threw a piece of egg. It landed on the floor. She laughed. "'Oops! Sorry, Gamma!'"

"That's okay, baby." Linda picked it up and smiled at her. Then she looked at me. "Grace is happy when you're here. Really here. Not half-distracted, not thinking about Margaret or Tyler or revenge. Just here."

"I am here."

"Are you?" Linda's voice was gentle. "Because every time your phone buzzes, you jump. Every time you look at your laptop, I see you thinking about going back."

She was right. Even now, sitting at the table with Grace, part of me was in New York, waiting for Keller's call and wondering what came next.

My phone buzzed. Keller.

We need to talk. Can you come to the office this afternoon?

My stomach dropped. This was it. The firing. The final humiliation. Linda saw my face. "What is it?"

"Keller wants to meet."

"Are you going?"

I looked at Grace. She was eating her eggs, humming to herself. Content. Safe. Then I looked at Linda. Her face was patient, waiting for me to decide. "I don't know," I said. "Should I?"

"That's not for me to answer." Linda stood up and started clearing plates. "But I will say this: If you go, Grace will be fine. She'll miss you, but she'll be fine. She's resilient."

"But?"

"But if you go and then you stay... if this turns into another month, another fight, another excuse, then I don't know if she forgives that. Or if I do."

She walked to the sink and turned on the water. "So you need to decide. Are you going to New York to get fired? Or are you going because you're not done fighting?"

I stared at my phone. Keller's message was waiting. Grace was humming in her high chair, and Linda was washing dishes, her back to me. "I have to go," I said finally. "Even if it's just to hear him fire me. I need to know."

"Okay." Linda turned off the water. "But you come home tonight, no matter what. You promise me that."

"I promise."

Linda dried her hands and walked over, touching my cheek. "I hope you're making the right choice."

"Me too."

I booked the cheapest flight I could find: a noon departure out of Cleveland for sixty-eight dollars one way. It would get me to LaGuardia by 1:30.

The airport was nearly empty. Tuesday afternoon. Just business travelers with their rolling suitcases and tired eyes.

People who did this every week. People who'd learned how to leave without feeling like they were abandoning everything that mattered.

I sat at the gate watching planes take off, watching them disappear into clouds. Wondering if one day I'd just disappear too. If Grace would even notice. If she'd care. The flight boarded. I found my seat. Middle row between a businessman who typed furiously and a college kid who slept through takeoff.

I stared out the tiny window as we climbed, watching Ohio disappear below. All those houses. All those lives. All those people who probably had their shit together better than I did.

The plane landed at 1:47. I took a taxi to Titan Capital and arrived at 2:30. I took the elevator to the 42nd floor. Miranda was waiting in the lobby. Her face was unreadable, as if she'd practiced how to deliver bad news and was trying to remember her lines.

"He's waiting for you."

We walked to Keller's office in silence. She knocked and opened the door. Keller sat at his desk, maintaining the same intimidating presence and cold eyes that seemed to see through everything. But something was different. He looked tired, as if the fight had cost him something too.

"Sit," he said.

I sat. Miranda closed the door and stood against it, blocking my escape route, as if I might run when I heard what was coming.

"I'm sorry," I said before either of them could speak. "I froze at the meeting. I cost us BlackRock. I understand if you want me to leave."

Keller studied me. A long silence followed, the kind that makes every second feel like an hour. Then he said, "You didn't cost us BlackRock. Margaret did."

I stared at him.

"She outplayed us," he continued. His voice was calm, but there was something underneath, something almost like respect. "She fired Tyler before we could even finish the presentation. Positioned herself as the hero cleaning up her son's mess. Made our entire strategy irrelevant in one move."

He leaned back in his chair. "I've been doing this for twenty years: hostile takeovers, proxy fights, corporate warfare. I've gone up against some of the smartest, most ruthless people in finance." He paused. "And I've never seen anyone move that fast, that decisively, that perfectly."

"So what does that mean?"

"It means Margaret Carrington is the most dangerous opponent I've ever faced." He smiled, but it wasn't a friendly smile; it was the smile of someone who'd just figured out a puzzle and liked what they found. "And it means I want her even more now than I did before."

My heart started pounding.

"Now?" I asked carefully. "You mean we're continuing?"

"Continuing?" Keller laughed, short and sharp. "We're just getting started."

He pulled up a document on his screen and turned it toward me. "Margaret's filing amended financial statements in thirty days, restating three years of revenue and taking a massive write-down to correct Tyler's fraud."

I looked at the numbers. They were brutal.

"The stock will crash," I said.

"Exactly. When investors see the real numbers, not Tyler's inflated bullshit, they'll panic. The stock could drop another forty to fifty percent."

Miranda stepped forward. "And when it does, we buy more. Double our position. Get to thirty percent ownership."

My chest tightened.

"I can't afford to buy more. I'm barely holding my current position. If there's another margin call—"

"That's why I'm making you an offer." Keller pulled out a document and slid it across the desk. I looked down.

Personal Loan Guarantee Agreement. Three million dollars.

"What is this?"

"Protection. If the stock drops and triggers a margin call, I'll personally guarantee the loan to keep you solvent. You'll maintain your ten percent position throughout this entire fight, no matter what happens to the stock price."

I stared at the numbers. Three million dollars. More money than I'd ever seen in my life.

"Why would you do that?"

"Because I need you in this. Skin in the game. Ten percent ownership makes you a legitimate shareholder. It gives us standing to sue. It provides us leverage that money alone can't buy." He tapped the document.

"Without you, we're just another activist investor causing trouble. With you, we're a coalition of shareholders fighting fraud. It changes the optics. It changes everything."

"But if the stock crashes and I can't pay it back—"

"Then I absorb the loss. You walk away free. No debt. No obligation." He paused. "Consider it my investment in taking down Margaret Carrington."

Miranda pulled up another document on her tablet. "The SEC is investigating. Margaret admitted she knew about the fraud for six months. Even if she claims she 'fixed it,' she still violated disclosure requirements. She should have informed investors immediately. She didn't. That's a different kind of fraud."

"Securities fraud," I said slowly.

"Exactly." Miranda's smile was sharp. "Tyler committed accounting fraud. Margaret committed disclosure fraud by covering it up. Different crimes. But crimes nonetheless."

Keller stood and walked to the window overlooking Manhattan. Forty-two floors up. The city spread out below like a game board. "Margaret showed her hand," he said. "She revealed that she knew. That she was complicit. That she protected Tyler even while knowing he was destroying the company." He turned back to me. "That's vulnerability. That's exposure. And we're going to use it."

This was bigger than I'd thought. Bigger than Tyler. Bigger than revenge.

"Here's what happens next," Keller continued. "You sign this guaranteed loan. You keep your ten percent position no matter what. And we file a shareholder derivative lawsuit against Margaret personally."

"For what?"

"Failure to disclose. Breach of fiduciary duty. Destroying shareholder value." He paused. "We go after Margaret. Not Tyler. Margaret."

My heart was racing now.

"Tyler was always small," I said quietly.

"Yes." Keller's eyes locked on mine. "You were right about that from the beginning. Margaret's the real target. She always has been."

He pulled out an envelope and handed it to me. "Your payment. Fifty thousand dollars as agreed. Plus a bonus. Another fifty thousand for your work so far."

I just stared at him. "But we lost."

"You did the work. You built the fraud case. You present-ed to BlackRock. The loss wasn't your fault." He paused. "And I need you to stay on the team. This bonus ensures you can afford to."

One hundred thousand dollars. More money than I'd made in two years at Parker Media.

"There's something else," Miranda said quietly. She pulled out another folder, thicker than the others. "The evidence about Leo. About Margaret's clubs. About the gangs."

My breath stopped. Everything in the room went still, as if the air itself were holding its breath.

"We've been investigating," Miranda continued. Her voice was gentle now. Careful, like she was handling something fragile. "Following the money from Carrington Media. And we found something."

She opened the folder and showed me financial records: bank transfers, shell companies, money flowing from Carrington subsidiaries to nightclub operations in three cities, including Millfield.

"Club Vertical was one of six clubs Margaret used for money laundering. But here's what you didn't know." She pulled out another document. "The laundering started in 2013, not 2015, like we thought. Two years earlier."

My hands started shaking.

"That means—"

"That means the gang infrastructure was already in place when Leo was killed in 2014." Miranda's voice was soft. "We can't prove a direct connection. The gang that killed Leo didn't leave clear evidence linking them to Margaret's clubs. But the infrastructure was there: Margaret's money, Margaret's operations, Margaret's empire."

I stared at the documents, at the proof that Margaret had funded the ecosystem that swallowed my brother whole.

"How do we prove it?" My voice came out broken. "How do we prove she's responsible for Leo?"

"We don't. Not criminally. The connections are too indirect, too many degrees of separation." Miranda paused. "But we can prove the money laundering, the RICO violations, the organized crime connections. That's federal prison time: twenty years minimum."

Keller sat back down and leaned forward on his desk. "Initially, we didn't want to pursue the criminal angle. Federal investigations take years. SEC violations are faster, cleaner. We could force Margaret out as CEO through shareholder pressure alone."

"But?" I could hear the shift in his voice.

"But after losing BlackRock, we need more pressure. More leverage." His eyes were hard now. "So here's the new strategy. We threaten to expose everything unless Margaret steps down: the money laundering, the gang connections, the RICO violations. We give it all to the FBI unless she walks away quietly."

"That's blackmail."

"That's negotiation." Keller's voice was ice cold. "She destroyed your life. Her money helped kill your brother. She covered up her son's crimes, protected gangs and fraudsters, and built an empire on blood money." He paused. "You think she deserves mercy?"

I thought about Leo, about the warehouse where he died, about seven years of no justice.

I thought about Margaret's face in that hotel room: cold, calculating. *I've always known. About the fraud. About the women. About all of it.* I thought about Tyler walking free, about Margaret still powerful, about the Carrington empire still standing while my brother rotted in the ground.

"No," I said quietly. "She doesn't deserve mercy."

"Good." Keller pushed the loan guarantee toward me and placed a pen on top. "Then sign this. Keep your position. Stay in the fight. And when you come back from Ohio, we destroy Margaret Carrington together."

I looked at the document: three million dollars of protection, the thing that would keep me in New York, keep me away from Grace. I picked up the pen, Linda's voice in my head: *Are you going to New York to get fired? Or are you going because you're not done fighting?* I put the pen down. "I need time to think."

Keller's face went cold. "Are you kidding? This is a no-brainer. You will lose millions."

"I know. But I need to talk to my family first."

"I won't wait long. The offer expires soon." His voice was flat. "And Margaret wins."

"I understand."

I grabbed my bag and left before either of them could respond. The unsigned document felt like fire in my bag the entire flight home. Three million dollars of protection. Or three million dollars of chains. I'd have to decide soon. But tonight, I just needed to see Grace and figure out if I was brave enough to choose her.

I caught the 7 PM flight back to Cleveland. The plane felt like a coffin. Too small. Too quiet. Everyone around me was reading or sleeping or pretending their lives weren't falling apart. Mine was. I pressed my forehead against the cold window and watched the lights below. Thousands of them. Millions. Each one a person who probably knew which direction they were heading. I didn't.

I landed at 8:30. The airport smelled like burned coffee and anxiety. My hands shook as I ordered an Uber. The driver didn't talk. Thank God. He just drove through streets I'd known my whole life. Past the high school where Leo dropped out. Past the warehouse district where they'd found his body. Past every ghost I'd been running from for seven years.

We pulled up to Linda's house at 9:11 PM. The porch light was on. Yellow. Waiting. I paid the driver, got out, and stood on the sidewalk staring at the house. Through the kitchen window, I could see Linda sitting at the table. Not moving. Just sitting. Like she'd been there for hours. Like she knew I'd come but wasn't sure I'd stay.

My legs didn't want to move. Didn't want to walk up those steps and face what came next. But I did it anyway. The door was unlocked. It always was. Small-town trust that should've died with Leo but somehow survived.

Linda looked up when I walked in. Her face was tired. So tired. Lines I hadn't noticed before. Gray hair she hadn't bothered to dye. A woman who'd buried her husband and one child and was watching me slowly kill the other one.

"How'd it go?"

Three words. But they carried the weight of everything. I set my bag down, my coat, my keys, like I was shedding pieces of myself.

"They still want me." My voice came out hollow. Empty. "They're going after Margaret now. Not Tyler. Margaret."

Linda's face didn't change. Didn't flinch. Like she'd already known. Like she'd been preparing for this answer since I left.

"For how long?"

"I don't know. Could be months."

"And Grace?"

The question hung there. Sharp. Cutting.

"I don't know what to do."

Linda closed her eyes. Took a long, slow breath. When she opened them, they were wet. "Do you want justice for Leo?"

"Yes." The word came out broken.

"Do you want Grace to have her mother?"

"Yes."

"Those might not be compatible things, Olivia." Linda's voice cracked on my name. "You might have to choose."

"I know."

"What are you going to do?"

I looked at my hands. They were shaking. Had been shaking since the meeting. Since Margaret threatened Grace. "I don't know."

Linda stood up, walked to the sink, and stood there with her back to me. Her shoulders rigid. Holding everything in.

"Grace is asking for you. She woke up." Her voice became softer. Sadder. "Go sit with her while you figure it out."

Then she walked past me, down the hall, to her bedroom, and closed the door without looking back.

I stood alone in the kitchen. The house was so quiet I could hear the refrigerator humming, the clock ticking, and my own heartbeat too loud in my ears. I walked to Grace's room. Each step felt heavier than the last. Like I was walking toward something I couldn't come back from. I opened the door. Grace was sitting up in her crib, thumb in her mouth, eyes catching the light from the hallway.

"Mama?"

The word gutted me.

"Hi, baby." I went to her and picked her up. She was so warm, so solid, so real. "I'm here."

"You came back."

Three words. But they meant she'd been worried I wouldn't. That she'd learned to expect me to leave.

"I promised I would."

She put her head on my shoulder, her breath warm against my neck, her little hand clutching my shirt like she was afraid I'd disappear.

"Mama stay?"

My throat closed. "For tonight, yes."

"Tomorrow?"

"Tomorrow too."

"And tomorrow tomorrow?"

"I don't know, sweetheart."

She pulled back and looked at me with those eyes. Too old. Too knowing. Three years old and already learning that promises break. "When you know, you tell me?"

"I'll tell you. I promise."

She settled against me. Safe. Trusting. Despite everything. And I held her, breathed in her shampoo smell, felt her heartbeat against mine, memorized the weight of her, the warmth, the way she fit perfectly in my arms.

My phone buzzed. Once. Twice. Grace's breathing had already slowed, even, asleep. I almost didn't check it. Almost threw the phone across the room. But I didn't.

I laid Grace back in her crib. Gently. So gently. She didn't wake. Just curled into herself, thumb finding her mouth. Safe without me.

I pulled out my phone. Unknown number.

You lost. Margaret won by using your daughter against you. Go home, Olivia. Grace needs you more than Leo needs justice. Some battles aren't worth winning. Let this one go.

I stared at the words. This text was telling me to stop. Telling me to choose Grace. I set the phone down and looked at my daughter sleeping. This was the answer. Right here. In this room. This child who needed me more than ghosts did.

I should turn off my phone, climb into bed, and wake up tomorrow to tell Keller I was done. Then another text came through.

But if you can't let it go, you should know something. The warehouse where Leo died has a storage unit #23. The police never checked it. There might be evidence still there about who really ordered the hit, about Margaret's involvement. The combination is Leo's death date: 0-4-1-8. If you go, go alone. And go tonight. By morning, it'll be gone.

My heart stopped. Storage unit. Evidence. The truth I'd been searching for seven years. This was a trap. It had to be. Margaret was sending me to the place where Leo died, setting me up. Waiting. But what if it wasn't? What if this was real?

Another text:

Leo was wearing his Ohio State hoodie when they killed him. The gray one with the red block O. You gave it to him for his 18th birthday. He never took it off. Even at the end, he was wearing a piece of you. Thought you'd want to know that.

My hands started shaking so hard I almost dropped the phone. The hoodie. I'd forgotten about the hoodie. But suddenly I could see it. Leo on his eighteenth birthday, standing in Linda's kitchen. That smile when he opened the box. The way he pulled it on immediately. Too big. Sleeves covering his hands. But he'd worn it anyway.

"Thanks, Livvy. It's perfect."

And he'd died in it, wearing a piece of me while I was deleting his texts and choosing my thesis over his life. I looked at Grace. Sleeping. Safe. Then at my phone. The address of the storage facility glowing on the screen.

Fifteen minutes away. Maybe less. If I went, I might find evidence. If I didn't go, I'd never know. I reached for my bag. My hands were shaking. My breath was coming too fast.

I pulled out Grandpa's compass. The brass was cold. Heavy. The crack running through the glass like a scar. I held it in my palm, watching the needle spin, searching. Searching. Never settling. And now I was about to follow this compass.

North was Grace. I knew that. I could feel it. Every cell in my body screamed that north was this room, this child, this life. But Leo's voice was calling from that warehouse.

Come get me, Livvy. Like you promised.

I closed my eyes. Saw his face. Eighteen years old. Wearing my sweatshirt. Smiling. Saw his body. The morgue. Gray. Cold. Dead. I grabbed my coat from the hook and walked out of Grace's room, down the hallway, past Linda's closed door, through the kitchen where I'd sat a thousand times. Out into the cold March night.

Linda's car was in the driveway, the engine cold. I slid behind the wheel. The seat was still warm from her body heat. Her rosary was hanging from the rearview mirror, swinging and catching the moonlight. I started the engine and looked back at the house one last time.

The porch light was still on. Yellow. Waiting. Grace's window was dark. She was sleeping. She wouldn't know I was gone until morning. By then, it might be too late. I put the car in drive and drove toward the warehouse district, toward Leo's death, toward whatever was waiting for me in storage unit #23.

My hands were shaking on the wheel, my breath fogging the windshield, my heart pounding so hard it hurt. I knew I might not come back. Knew Grace might wake up tomorrow and I'd be gone. Knew Linda would have to explain to a three-year-old why Mama left in the middle of the night and never came home. Just like she'd explained Leo's death to me.

I drove faster. The warehouse district rose up ahead. Dark. Empty. Waiting. I should turn around. I knew that. Should go home, climb into bed next to Grace, wake up and tell Keller I was done. But I didn't. I kept driving. They were just gravity, and I'd been falling toward this moment since the day Leo died.

Chapter Nine

Where Leo Died

THE WAREHOUSE DISTRICT LOOKED like a graveyard for broken dreams. I drove through streets I'd known my whole life, past the high school where Leo dropped out. The windows were still boarded up from budget cuts, past Morrison's Grocery, where we'd both bagged groceries after school. Still there. Still barely surviving. Past all the places we'd lived before everything fell apart.

The GPS led me down Fifth Street. Industrial buildings lined both sides, broken windows like knocked-out teeth. Graffiti screamed things nobody wanted to hear. Weeds pushed through cracked pavement as if the earth was trying to reclaim what humans had abandoned. This was where Leo had died. I could feel it. The wrongness. The death that had soaked into the concrete here.

The storage facility sat at the end of the block. The chain-link fence sagged in the middle. The rusted gate hung open. An invitation. Or a warning.

I parked Linda's car on the street. The engine ticked as it cooled. My hands froze on the wheel. This was wrong. Everything about this was wrong. I should turn around, go home, wake up Grace, tell her I'd made the right choice for once. But I didn't.

I got out. The air hit me. Cold. Sharp. Smelling like oil and rust and something rotten underneath. My legs moved without permission, carrying me toward the gate, toward the storage units, toward whatever was waiting.

Storage Unit 23 sat in the back row. An orange door. A combination lock hung like a dare. My hands shook as I reached for it.

0-4-1-8.

April 18th. The day Leo died. The numbers spun under my fingers. Each click felt final, like I was unlocking more than just a door.

The lock opened. I pulled the door up. It screeched. Metal on metal. The sound echoed off empty buildings. Too loud. Too final. Like a scream that nobody would hear. Inside was dark. Completely dark. I fumbled for my phone. The screen light barely penetrated. Empty except for a cardboard box in the center.

Perfect placement. Like someone had staged it. Like this was theater. My heart pounded so hard it hurt. This was it. The evidence. The truth about Leo, about Margaret, about everything.

I stepped inside. The door slammed shut behind me. Metal clanged. The lock clicked. I spun around, trying to lift the door. Locked from the outside.

"Hello?" My voice came out small. Thin. The voice of a scared child. Footsteps. Multiple. Coming from the darkness. They'd been waiting—in the corners, in the shadows. The whole time. Then hands, grabbing me from everywhere. Strong hands. Male hands. Too many to fight.

I screamed, tried to twist away, but there were too many. Something rough went over my head. Burlap maybe. Scratchy, smelling like mildew and old dirt. I couldn't see. My arms were wrenched behind my back. Plastic cut into my wrists. Zip ties. The sound of them tightening. The bite of them cutting off circulation.

I was dragged outside, my feet stumbling over gravel. Hands gripped my arms hard enough to bruise, hard enough to leave marks I'd see for weeks. I was shoved into a vehicle. A van. I heard the door slide, smelled diesel and cigarettes, felt the floor vibrating beneath me.

The door slammed, and the engine started. We were moving. I couldn't see, couldn't move my hands, couldn't breathe properly through the bag. Each breath pulled in fabric, making me choke, making me panic.

My brain was screaming. This is how I die. This is how Grace loses her mother. This is the pattern completing itself. Time lost all meaning. Could've been five minutes, could've been an hour. Just darkness, engine noise, and my own ragged breathing. Then the van stopped. Silence for a moment, then the door slid open.

Cold air rushed in. Hands grabbed me again, dragging me out. My feet hit gravel, and I stumbled. They held me up and walked me forward. I tried to count steps, tried to remember turns, tried to leave breadcrumbs for someone to follow. But there was no one following.

We stopped, and hands forced me down to my knees. Concrete. Cold. Rough. The texture somehow familiar. The bag came off. Light flooded in. Streetlight. Moon. Enough to see. And I knew exactly where I was: behind the warehouse on Fifth Street, the exact spot where Leo died.

The dark stain and blood on the concrete were gone now, but I could still see it somehow. Maybe a hallucination. Right in front of me. Seven years of rain and sun and people walking past without knowing, without caring. But still there. Leo's blood. And I was kneeling right next to it, my knees where his knees had been, my body where his body had fallen.

"No," I whispered. "No, no, no."

Then I felt it. Cold metal pressed against the back of my head. Hard. Deliberate. Unmistakable.

A gun. Everything stopped. My heart. My breath. Time itself.

This was it. This was how I died. In the same place as Leo, the same way as Leo. My whole life flashed before me. Not slowly, but fast. Too fast to hold onto.

Six years old. Bathroom floor. Cold tile under my knees. Dad's voice through the door. Slurred. Angry. Making a promise: never be like Daddy. Never, ever, ever. A promise I'd spent my entire life breaking in different ways.

Eight years old. Teaching Leo about footsteps. Heavy and uneven means danger; light and even means safe. His little hand in mine, blue eyes looking up, trusting me to keep him safe. Promise, Livvy? Promise, baby brother.

Fourteen. Finding Leo drunk for the first time. Twelve years old with vodka on his breath. Already becoming Dad. Already lost. Me doing nothing, choosing straight A's over saving him, choosing future over family.

Twenty-one. The texts I deleted. Leo's last words: "They found me. I love you, sis." Deleted while brushing my teeth, choosing thesis over life, choosing convenience over love.

The morgue. Leo's face. Gray. Waxy. Not him anymore. Cold hands that used to hold mine. I realized I had $8,247 sitting in my bank account. Coffee money. Security deposit money. His life was worth less than my comfort.

Twenty-two. Peninsula Hotel. Tyler's hand on my wine glass when I wasn't looking. The room spinning. The scarves. The pain. Grace conceived in violence. A daughter born from rape.

Linda holding newborn Grace. "She's beautiful. Your daughter is beautiful." Grace screaming in the NICU. Tiny chest rising and falling with machines helping. Proof that sometimes broken things survive if someone fights for them.

Grace learning to walk. Falling. Getting up. Falling. Getting up. Never giving up. Never learning to quit. Showing me what strength looks like.

All of it. Every moment. Every choice. Every promise made and broken. Twenty-eight years of trying to outrun my father's ghost. And now it was ending here. Where Leo's ended. His blood under my knees. His terror in my chest. His last thoughts in my head. Except there was nobody left to call for. Leo had called for me.

I had nobody.

"You were warned." The voice behind me was cold. Professional. Male. Midwest accent. "In your hotel room. At the BlackRock meeting. Margaret Carrington told you to leave. Told you what would happen if you didn't listen."

I couldn't speak. Couldn't breathe. Could barely think past the gun against my skull.

"This is the warehouse where Leo Parker died. April 18th, 2014. Right here. This exact spot." The voice was matter-of-fact. Reciting facts. "He was on his knees. Just like you. Gun to his head. Just like you."

Tears streamed down my face. Soaking into my shirt. Dripping onto Leo's bloodstain.

"He was calling for you. 'Livvy will save me.' That's what he kept saying. Over and over. Your name. Like a prayer. Like if he said it enough times, you'd magically appear."

Oh God. Oh God, please no.

"But you didn't come." The voice got quieter. Almost gentle. "And he died here. Alone. Terrified."

I was sobbing now. My whole body shaking. Snot and tears mixing. Not caring about dignity. Past caring about anything.

"Margaret wanted you to understand something." The gun pressed harder. "She could've done this anywhere. Your hotel room. Your car. Your mother's house while your daughter slept down the hall."

The thought of Grace twisted my stomach.

"But she wanted you here. Where Leo died. So you'd know exactly what he felt in his last moments."

My mind raced, trying to memorize details. Trying to collect evidence. The voice. Familiar somehow. Midwest accent. Professional. Like a lawyer or businessman.

The gun. Cold. Metal. Felt like a 9mm. Standard. Nothing unique. The men. At least three. Maybe four. All bigger than me. Trained movements. Military maybe. Or the same gangs who killed Leo. But what did it matter? If I died here, the evidence died with me.

"Do you feel it? Do you understand now what your brother felt?" The voice paused. I thought about Grace. My baby girl. Three years old. I reflected on all the promises I'd made.

"Say goodbye, Ms. Parker." The voice was almost gentle now. Almost kind. "Go to where your brother is."

I closed my eyes. I saw Grace's face. Sleeping. Trusting me to be there in the morning. I saw Linda's face. Disappointed. Not surprised. She'd known I'd choose wrong. I saw Leo's face. Eighteen years old. Smiling. Wearing my hoodie. I waited for the bullet. I waited for everything to end.

CLICK.

The hammer fell. But no explosion. No bullet. No death. No brain matter spraying across Leo's bloodstain. Just a click. Empty chamber.

My heart stopped. Then started again. Wrong rhythm. Too fast. Like it was trying to escape my chest. I couldn't process it. Couldn't understand. Dead but not dead. Gone but still here.

"No bullet," the voice said. "Not this time."

I couldn't stop shaking. Couldn't stop crying. Couldn't make my brain work properly. The gun lifted away from my head. Cool air rushed to fill the space where death had been.

"Margaret wants you to understand what we're capable of." Footsteps. Walking away. "This was a warning. Next time, there will be a bullet in the chamber. Next time, we pull the trigger."

More footsteps. Multiple people leaving. A van engine starting in the distance. "Go home to your daughter. Stop looking. Stop fighting." The voice was farther away now. "Or next time, you won't leave this warehouse."

Then silence. Just wind. And me. And Leo's bloodstain.

I don't know how long I stayed there. On my knees. Sobbing. Shaking. Couldn't move. Couldn't think. Couldn't do anything but replay that click over and over.

The moment I thought I was going to die. The moment I felt exactly what Leo felt. My hands were still zip-tied behind my back. But looser now. They'd cut them partially. Enough that I could work free. I pulled. The plastic cut into my wrists. Drew blood. The pain felt distant. Unimportant compared to the gun that had been against my head. Finally, they came free. I ripped off what was left of the bag. Threw it away from me.

Alone. Behind the warehouse. In the dark. The exact spot where Leo knelt seven years ago. Where he'd called my name. Where he'd died believing I would come. And I'd just knelt there. With a gun to my head. Feeling exactly what he felt.

I stood up. My legs were shaking so badly I had to lean against the warehouse wall. Brick rough against my palms. Solid. Real. Proof I was still alive. I found my way back to the street. Linda's car was still there. Keys in the ignition. Phone on the passenger seat.

They'd brought me in a circle. Back to where I started. No witnesses. No cameras in this dead neighborhood. No proof except my bloody wrists and trauma.

I got in the car, locked the doors, and sat there shaking. My phone lit up. Unknown number.

There was never any evidence about Leo. That was the trap. Margaret wanted you to know she can reach you anywhere. Anytime. She can make you disappear, and nobody would ever know what happened. Stop looking. Stop fighting. Or next time is real.

I stared at the message. My hands were shaking so hard I could barely hold the phone. This was kidnapping. Assault. Attempted murder maybe, or at least terroristic threats. I should call 911, report it, get police here, get evidence, get protection. But even as I thought it, I knew why I wouldn't.

No witnesses. No cameras. Just me and my story: me, the alcoholic prostitute with a vendetta versus Margaret, the respected CEO cleaning up her son's mess. Who would they believe? And if I reported it, what would stop Margaret from finishing the job? Next time with a real bullet? I deleted the message, started the car, and drove home.

Every red light felt like it lasted forever. Every shadow looked like someone waiting to grab me. Every car behind me felt like it was following. Every turn could be another trap. I couldn't stop shaking. Couldn't stop seeing that bloodstain. Couldn't stop feeling that gun against my head.

CLICK. The sound kept echoing over and over. The hammer falling on an empty chamber. The moment between life and death. The moment I understood Leo.

I got home at 2:47 AM, around the same time as Leo's last call to me seven years ago. The synchronicity felt deliberate, like Margaret had planned even that. Linda was still asleep. Grace was still asleep. The house was quiet, warm, and safe, like nothing had happened. But everything had happened.

I went to the bathroom and looked at myself in the mirror. My wrists were bleeding where the zip ties had cut. My face was streaked with tears and dirt. My eyes were wild, haunted, animalistic. I looked exactly like Leo probably looked that night, seven years ago, when he was running, hiding, calling me for help, and I'd sent him to voicemail.

Now I knew what that felt like: the calling for someone who doesn't come, the understanding that you're going to die and there's nothing you can do.

I washed my face, wrapped my wrists with gauze from the medicine cabinet, changed my clothes, and put the bloody ones in a plastic bag, stuffing it deep in the kitchen trash under coffee grounds and eggshells. No evidence. Like it never happened. Except it did happen, and I would never forget it: the feel of that gun, the sound of that click, the moment I thought I was dead.

I went to my room, sat on the bed, and stared at the wall as light crept across the floor. I kept thinking. Just give up on Leo. Give up on justice. Give up on making Margaret pay for what she'd done.

I sat there until the sun came up. Until I heard Grace stirring. Until Linda's footsteps in the hallway. I was trying to decide if I was brave enough to keep fighting after Margaret had shown me exactly what she was capable of. Or smart enough to walk away before the next chamber had a bullet in it.

My phone rang at 7:47 AM. Miranda. I stared at it. Three rings. Four. I knew I should answer. I knew I couldn't explain. On the fifth ring, I picked up.

"Hello?"

"Olivia." Her voice was sharp. Urgent. "Where were you last night?"

My throat closed. "What?"

"I tried calling you at midnight. And 2 AM. And 4 AM. Your phone was off. Linda said you weren't home. Where were you?"

I looked at my bandaged wrists. The blood seeping through the gauze. "I went out."

"Where?"

"I can't—" My voice cracked. "I can't talk about it."

Silence on the other end. Then: "What happened?"

"Nothing. I'm fine."

"You're not fine. I can hear it in your voice." Miranda's tone changed. Softer. "Talk to me. Please."

The whole night came flooding back. The gun. The click. Leo's blood. "I got a text," I whispered. "About evidence. About Leo. A storage unit where he died."

"Oh no." Miranda's voice dropped. "Olivia, tell me you didn't—"

"They were waiting." The words came out broken. "Zip ties. Bag over my head. Drove me somewhere. Put me on my knees where Leo died." I couldn't stop now. Couldn't hold it in. "Gun to my head. They pulled the trigger. Empty chamber. A warning."

"Jesus Christ." I heard movement on her end. Papers rustling. A door closing. "We need to call the police. Right now. This is kidnapping. Assault. This is—"

"No." The word came out sharp. Final.

"What do you mean no? Olivia, this is a major felony. We can—"

"We can what?" I stood up. Started pacing. "Tell the police that Margaret Carrington, respected CEO, worth hundreds of millions, kidnapped me? With what proof? My story?"

"Your injuries—"

"Could be from anything. Self-harm. An accident. I have a history of mental health issues, remember? Margaret made sure everyone at BlackRock knew that."

Silence. Then: "Fuck."

"Yeah."

"It's your word against hers," Miranda said slowly, understanding dawning. "And you're—"

"An alcoholic sex worker with a vendetta. Yeah." I laughed, but it came out broken. "She's a pillar of the community, cleaning up her son's mess. Who do you think they'll believe?"

"But there has to be something we can do—"

"Like what?" My voice was rising now. Getting hysterical. "Report it and give her a reason to finish the job? Next time with a real bullet? Or maybe she goes after Grace instead. Or Linda."

"Olivia—"

"She can reach me anywhere, Miranda. That's what last night was about. Showing me she can make me disappear, and nobody would ever know what happened." I was crying now. I couldn't stop. "So no. We're not calling the police. We're not reporting anything. Because that's how I end up actually dead instead of just scared."

Miranda was quiet for a long time. I could hear her breathing. Processing. "So she gets away with it."

"She gets away with everything." I wiped my eyes. "That's what power means. She can kidnap me. Threaten me. Make me kneel where my brother died. And there's nothing I can do about it."

"There has to be—"

"There isn't." I cut her off. "Unless you can think of a way to prove it. To get evidence. To make it stick. Otherwise, reporting it just gives her a reason to silence me permanently."

More silence. Then: "I'm so sorry."

"Yeah. Me too."

"What are you going to do?"

"I don't know."

"Keller wants an answer about the loan guarantee by the end of the day." Her voice was gentle now. Professional mask back on. "Whether you're staying in or selling out."

I looked at my bandaged wrists. I felt the ghost of that gun against my head. I heard that click echoing in my memory.

"I need time to think."

"You don't have time. If you don't sign, Keller can't protect your position." She paused. "Look, I know what you're thinking. But Olivia? We can't just stop fighting here because of the threat. That's exactly what Margaret wants."

"Is that what you'd do if you were me?"

Long silence. Then: "I don't know. I've never had someone put a gun to my head."

"Lucky you."

"I need your answer by five." Her voice was sad. "I'm sorry. I wish there were another way."

"Yeah. Me too."

She hung up. I stood there holding my phone, staring at nothing. Linda appeared in the doorway, Grace in her arms. Still sleepy. Hair sticking up.

"Mama!" Grace reached for me.

I took her. Held her. Breathed in her shampoo smell. Felt her heartbeat against mine.

"Who was that?" Linda asked.

"Work."

Linda looked at my wrists, my face, my eyes that couldn't quite focus. She knew something had happened. "What did you do?" Not accusatory. Just sad. Like she'd been expecting this.

"Made another wrong choice."

"Are you going to keep making them?"

I held Grace tighter. "I don't know." Grace pulled back and looked at my bandages. Her little fingers reached out to touch them gently.

"Mama hurt?"

"A little bit."

"I kiss it?" She leaned forward and pressed her lips to the gauze. "Better now."

Her breath was warm against my wrist. Her kiss was so gentle, so full of love and trust and belief that she could fix things. I had until five o'clock to decide if I was willing to risk finding out the hard way.

Grace settled against my chest, already falling back asleep. Safe. Trusting. Not knowing that her mother had almost died last night. Not knowing that next time, the chamber might not be empty.

Linda was still standing there, watching me, waiting for an answer I didn't have. "I'm making breakfast," she said finally. "You should eat something."

"I'm not hungry."

"You need to eat anyway." She turned toward the kitchen, stopped, and looked back at me. "Whatever you're deciding, Olivia, remember this: Grace needs her mother."

Then she was gone, leaving me alone with my daughter, my bandaged wrists, and the memory of that gun against my head. Leaving me to figure out if justice for Leo was worth dying for.

The phone in my hand felt heavy. Five o'clock. Seven hours to decide. Grace's breath was warm and even against my neck. I closed my eyes and tried to figure out which way was north when the compass was broken, the gun was loaded, and time was running out.

Chapter Ten

Hiding

I COULDN'T LEAVE THE house. Not after what happened. Not with my wrists still bandaged. Not with the feel of that gun still pressed against my skull.

Grace was in the kitchen with Linda. I could hear her through the walls. Singing. Playing. Happy sounds that felt like they were coming from another world.

I sat on my bed and stared at the clock. 9:47 AM. Miranda wanted an answer by 5 PM. Seven hours and thirteen minutes to decide.

My phone was off. Battery out. Hidden in my drawer. But I could still feel it. Still hear it buzzing even though it wasn't.

Keller wanted to know if I'd sign the guarantee. If I'd stay in the fight. But how could I fight when Margaret could reach me anywhere? When she'd shown me exactly what she was capable of? When she'd made me kneel where Leo died and pulled the trigger on an empty chamber? Next time it wouldn't be empty. I knew that. Believed it. Felt it in my bones.

Grace's voice drifted through the door. "Gamma, can we go to the park?"

"Maybe later, baby. Let's have breakfast first." Normal sounds. Safe sounds. The life I wanted. The life I'd almost lost last night.

I looked at my wrists. The bandages were clean now, but I could still see the blood in my mind. Still feel the zip ties cutting. Still smell that warehouse.

My phone was in the drawer. Waiting. I pulled it out. Stared at it. Put the battery back in. Turned it on. Thirty-seven missed calls. Sixty-two text messages. Most from Miranda. Some from Keller. A few from unknown numbers. The most recent text was from Miranda at 8:15 AM. *Please call me.*

We need to talk before 5. This is important.

My hands were shaking. I should call. Should explain. Should tell them I was done. But if I called, I'd have to say it out loud. Make it real. Admit I was giving up.

Another text came through while I was staring at the screen. Miranda again.

Olivia. I know you're scared. I know what happened was traumatic. But we need to discuss options. Please call me by noon.

Options. What options were there? Stay and fight and risk dying like Leo? Or quit and live and let Margaret win? Those were the only choices. And I'd already made mine. I'd chosen Grace. I started typing a response.

I can't do this anymore. I'm sorry. I'm done.

My finger hovered over send. Grace's voice again. Closer now. Right outside my door. "Mama? You awake?"

I deleted the message. Put the phone down. "Yeah, baby. I'm awake."

The door opened. Grace peeked in. Hair messy from sleep. Thumb in her mouth.

"Come play with me?"

"Of course."

She ran to me. Climbed into my lap. Warm and solid and real. This was what mattered. Not revenge. Not justice. Not a dead brother. This living child who needed her mother.

"What do you want to play?" I asked.

"Blocks. Build castle."

"Okay. Let's build a castle."

We went to the living room. She dumped out her blocks and started stacking.

"Mama help?"

I helped, building with her. Present. Focused. Pushing away thoughts of Margaret, warehouses, and guns. For twenty minutes, it worked. Then Linda's phone rang in the kitchen. I heard her answer and heard her voice change.

"She's here, but I don't know if she wants to—" Pause.

"I understand. Let me ask her." Linda appeared in the doorway, her face worried. "Miranda is on my phone. She says it's urgent."

My stomach dropped. "I don't—"

"She says if you don't talk to her by noon, Keller is making decisions without you."

Grace was still building, oblivious and happy. I didn't want to take the call. I didn't want to hear whatever Miranda had to say. But I also couldn't just ignore them. They controlled the guarantee that was protecting my position.

"I'll take it in my room."

Linda handed me her phone. "Be careful, baby."

I went back to my room, closed the door, and put the phone to my ear. "Hello?"

"Thank God." Miranda's voice was tight and stressed. "Where have you been?"

"Home."

"Your phone has been off for three hours."

"I needed space."

"We don't have space. The margin call is due tomorrow. Keller needs to know if you're signing the guarantee or if we're liquidating your position."

The words hit like stones.

"I can't—" My voice broke. "I can't do this anymore."

Silence on the other end.

"Margaret asked her people to put a gun to my head, Miranda. They made me kneel where Leo died. They pulled the trigger." My voice shook now. "Next time it won't be empty. And I have a three-year-old daughter who needs her mother."

"I know."

"So I'm done. I'm staying home. I'm choosing Grace."

More silence.

"I understand," Miranda said quietly. "I do. But Olivia, if you don't sign the guarantee, your position gets liquidated when the stock price drops."

"And Margaret wins," Miranda continued. "She terrorizes you into quitting. Gets away with everything. Leo gets no justice. The gangs that killed him face no consequences."

The words cut deep.

"I can't risk my life for revenge."

"I'm not asking you to." Miranda's voice changed and got sharper. "I'm asking you to consider an option you haven't thought about."

"What option?"

"Stay home. Don't come back to New York. Don't fight. Don't put yourself in danger." She paused. "But don't sell your shares."

"I don't understand."

"Keller and I were discussing this morning. If you're too afraid to fight but don't want to give up your position, there's a middle ground."

My heart was pounding. "What middle ground?"

"You keep your shares. Keller's loan guarantee protects you from the bank margin calls. Your 10% position stays intact."

"In exchange for what?"

"Complete voting proxy. You give Titan Capital the right to vote your shares however we want for the next two years. Irrevocable."

I sat down on the bed. "You want me to give up control of my shares."

"Yes."

"But keep the financial risk."

"And the financial upside. If we win, if Carrington Media gets turned around or sold, your shares could be worth twenty or thirty million. But you don't have to do anything. You stay home. Stay safe. Stay with Grace."

"And you and Keller use my votes to fight Margaret."

"Exactly."

I stared at the wall, processing. "So I hide while you do the fighting."

"You survive while we do the fighting," Miranda corrected. "There's no shame in that. Margaret tried to kill you last night. Nobody would blame you for stepping back."

"Except I'd still be in the game. Still a target."

"Maybe. But without you actively fighting, without you showing up to meetings or making presentations, Margaret has less reason to come after you." Miranda's voice softened. "You become a passive investor instead of an active threat. You're not worth the risk of another kidnapping."

It made sense. Horrible, cowardly sense. "What happens if you lose?" I asked. "If Margaret wins the proxy fight?"

"Then the value of your shares will depend on how Margaret runs her company and convinces investors. You may gain or lose money, but you're protected from margin calls. You won't go bankrupt."

"And if you win?"

"Then Margaret is out. New management takes over. The company gets sold or restructured. Your shares could triple, quadruple, or even increase significantly in value. We all make tons of money together."

I thought about Grace playing with blocks in the living room. Happy. Safe. I thought about Leo. Dead in a warehouse. Calling my name. Getting no answer. "How long do I have to decide?"

"Keller needs an answer by five today. Same deadline."

I looked at the clock. 10:23 AM. Six hours and thirty-seven minutes. "Can I think about it?"

"Of course. But Olivia?" Miranda's tone turned serious. "This is the only option where you keep your position and stay home. If you say no, the bank will liquidate your position after your stock drops. You lose your money, and Margaret knows she scared you into selling."

"She did scare me into selling."

"Then at least make her work for it. Give us your proxy. Let us fight. Stay home with Grace. And if we win, you win too. Leo gets justice, and you get to be Grace's mother."

She was right. I knew she was right.

"I'll call you back before five."

"Okay. And Olivia? I meant what I said earlier. Walking away isn't weakness. It's survival. Nobody will judge you for choosing Grace."

She hung up. I sat there holding Linda's phone. Six hours to decide. Give up control of my shares and hide while Keller and Miranda fought? Or sell everything and walk away completely? Either way, I wasn't fighting. Either way, I was choosing Grace. But one option kept me in the game. It kept the possibility of justice alive. And one option meant Margaret had won completely.

I went back to the living room. Grace had built a tower. Tall, wobbly, and proud.

"Look, Mama! Castle!"

"It's beautiful, baby."

"Can you help me make it taller?"

I sat down next to her and started stacking blocks. Linda was in the doorway, watching and waiting. "What did Miranda want?" she asked.

"Another option. Instead of selling."

"What kind of option?"

"Keep my shares but give them voting control. I stay home. They fight Margaret."

Linda's face was unreadable. "What do you think?"

"I don't know."

Grace knocked over the tower. Blocks scattered everywhere. She laughed. "Again! Build again!"

We built again, higher this time. But my mind wasn't on blocks. It was on the choice. Hide completely? Or hide strategically? Quit entirely? Or quit actively while staying passively involved?

"What would Leo want?" Linda asked quietly. The question stopped me. What would Leo want? Would he want me to risk my life for revenge? To die trying to get justice for him? Or would he want me to survive? To raise Grace? To break the pattern?

"I don't know," I whispered.

"Yes, you do." Linda came and sat next to us. "Leo loved you. He'd want you safe. He'd want Grace to have her mother."

"But would he want me to give up?"

"You're not giving up. You're choosing life over death. There's a difference."

Grace was humming, building, oblivious to the conversation happening over her head.

"If I give them voting control, I'm still a target," I said. "Margaret might come after me anyway."

"Maybe. But you'll be here. With me. With Grace. We'll keep you safe."

"Nobody kept Leo safe."

The words came out harsher than I meant. Linda flinched. "No. We didn't. But Leo was alone. You're not."

I thought about last night. The warehouse. The zip ties, the gun. Nobody had been there. Nobody had saved me. I'd survived because Margaret chose to let me survive. Next time, she might not.

"I'm scared," I admitted.

"Of course you are. She tried to kill you."

"She didn't try. She warned." I looked at my bandaged wrists. "Next time she'll finish it."

"Then don't give her a next time. Stay home. Stay hidden. Let Keller's team do the work."

"But I'll still own the shares. Still have a stake."

"A passive stake. You're not dangerous if you're not fighting." Linda touched my shoulder. "Baby, you can't win against someone like Margaret if she's willing to kill. You just can't. The only way to win is to survive."

Grace's tower fell again. This time she didn't laugh. She just looked at the scattered blocks. "Why falling, Mama?"

"Because we're building it too tall without a strong foundation."

She thought about that. "So shorter?"

"Or build it stronger."

She started rebuilding. Carefully this time. Making the base wider. More stable. I watched her work. Building it stronger. That's what I needed to do. Not taller. Not bigger. Just stronger. Strong enough to survive.

"I'm going to do it," I said. "Give them voting control. Keep the shares. Stay home."

Linda nodded slowly. "You sure?"

"No. But I'm sure I can't go back there. I can't risk dying like Leo." I looked at Grace. "She needs me more than Leo needs revenge."

"Okay then."

"You think I'm making the right choice?"

Linda was quiet for a moment, watching Grace build. "I think you're making the only choice that keeps you alive. Alive is better than dead. Even if it means Margaret wins."

"She doesn't win everything. Keller is still fighting."

"But you're not."

"No. I'm not."

The admission felt like surrender. Like giving up. But also like relief. Like choosing life instead of death. Like finally breaking the pattern.

I called Miranda back at 2:47 PM, three hours before the deadline. Grace was napping. Linda was in the garden. The house was quiet.

"I'll do it," I said when she answered. "I'll give you voting control."

"You're sure?"

"No. But I'm choosing Grace. And this is the best way to choose Grace without completely giving up."

"Okay." Miranda's voice was gentle. "I'll have the lawyers draft the proxy agreement. You'll need to sign it by tomorrow morning before the market opens."

"How do I sign it?"

"Electronic signature. I'll email you the documents. You review, sign digitally, and send them back."

"That's it?"

"That's it. Then Titan Capital controls your votes. You keep your shares. Keller's guarantee protects you from margin calls. You're locked in."

"For two years."

"Yes, two years. By then, this will be over. One way or another."

I thought about two years. Grace would be five. Maybe even starting kindergarten.

Two years of staying home. Being present. Building something stable. It sounded impossible. Like peace I didn't deserve.

"Send me the documents," I said. "I'll sign them tonight."

"Good."

She hung up. I sat there in the quiet house, holding the phone. Feeling the weight of the decision settle. I'd given up. Given in. Surrendered. But I'd also survived. Chosen Grace. Broken the pattern. Whether that was winning or losing, I didn't know yet. But I was alive to find out. And that had to count for something.

The documents arrived at 6:23 PM.

Irrevocable Proxy Agreement

I read through them. Legal language that basically stated: Olivia Parker gives Titan Capital Management complete voting control over her shares in Carrington Media for two years. In exchange, Titan Capital guarantees protection from margin calls up to $3 million.

I owned the shares. But I couldn't vote them. Couldn't control them. Couldn't do anything except watch. I was a passenger now, not a driver. My hand hovered over the signature box. This was it. The moment I gave up control. Gave up the fight. Chose hiding over fighting. Chose life over revenge.

Grace appeared in the doorway, rubbing her eyes, her hair messy from her nap. "Mama? What are you doing?"

"Just work stuff, baby."

"You working again?" The fear in her voice stopped me cold.

"No. Not like before. I'm just signing something. Then I'm done. I'm staying home."

She climbed onto my lap and watched the screen. "What's that?"

"It's a paper that says Mama doesn't have to go to work in New York anymore."

"Good." She snuggled against me. "I want you here."

"I want to be here too." I looked at the signature box, then at Grace, then back at the screen.

I clicked sign. The document processed. Submitted. Done. No going back now. My phone buzzed. Text from Miranda.

Received. You're locked in. Welcome to the passenger seat.

I put the phone down and held Grace.

"Story time?" she asked.

"Yeah, baby. Story time."

We went to her room. I read her three books. She fell asleep halfway through the third one. I stayed anyway, sitting on the edge of her bed, watching her breathe. Alive. Safe. Mine. Worth more than any revenge. Worth more than any fight.

Linda knocked softly on the doorframe. "You signed it?"

"Yeah. I'm officially a passive investor now."

"How do you feel?"

"Like a coward."

"You're not a coward. You're a mother."

"Can't I be both?"

"Maybe. But one matters more than the other." Linda came and sat next to me. "Leo would be proud of you for choosing Grace."

"You really think so?"

"I know so. Because he loved you. And he'd want you alive and happy more than he would want you dead and avenged."

I wanted to believe that. Wanted to believe Leo's ghost wasn't disappointed. Wasn't angry. Wasn't wondering why his sister had given up the fight.

"Margaret will still be under investigation," Linda said. "FBI. SEC. All of it. She's not getting away clean."

"But I'm not the one bringing her down."

"Does it matter who brings her down as long as she falls?"

I thought about that. Did it matter? Did I need to be the one to destroy Margaret? Did I need to see her face when she lost? Or could I live with knowing it happened without me?

"I don't know," I admitted.

"You will. Eventually." Linda stood up. "Come on. Let's have dinner. A normal dinner. As a family. Like we should've been doing all along."

"Okay."

We left Grace sleeping and went to the kitchen. Linda made spaghetti. We ate at the table and talked about nothing important: the weather, the garden, Grace's new favorite TV show.

Normal things. Safe things. It felt wrong, like I was betraying Leo by having a normal dinner. But it also felt right, like I was finally choosing the life I should've been living all along. After dinner, Linda hugged me.

"I'm proud of you," she whispered.

"I just hope it's enough."

"It is, baby. It is."

That night, I lay in bed staring at the ceiling, wondering if I'd made the right choice. My wrists still hurt. The bandages itched. The memory of that gun was still fresh. But I was alive. And Grace was asleep down the hall. That had to be enough. It had to be. Because I'd already given up everything else.

For the first three days, I didn't turn on my phone at all. I kept it in a drawer, battery out, as if it didn't exist. Grace and I went to the playground. I pushed her on the swing. We got ice cream. I read her books at night. Normal life. Safe life. Linda watched me carefully, waiting for the cracks to show.

On Day 4, I turned the phone on just to check the time. The notifications exploded: eighty-three messages, forty-seven missed calls. I told myself I'd just see what Miranda wanted. One quick look. I opened her message.

Stock crashed to $6.80 after amended statements. SEC opening investigation. Everything proceeding as planned.

My hands started shaking. $6.80. From $12.0 million down to $7.1 million. I'd lost nearly five million dollars in four days.

"Mama?" Grace was tugging my shirt. "Come play?"

"Yeah, baby. One second." But I was already opening the brokerage app, watching the numbers refresh. $6.75. $6.68. Still falling.

"Mama!"

"I said one second!"

The sharpness in my voice made her flinch. I put the phone down. "Sorry, baby. Let's play."

We played with blocks for maybe five minutes before I heard it buzz. Another message. I couldn't ignore it. That night, I read every article about Carrington Media. All forty-three of them.

Day 5 started at 3 AM. I woke up and couldn't fall back asleep. I grabbed my phone. The market wasn't even open, but I checked anyway. Checked news. Checked Reddit threads, checked everything.

At 6 AM, Grace climbed into my bed. She found me still scrolling. She didn't say anything. Just looked at the glowing screen, then at my face, and curled up next to me, facing away.

On Day 6, Grace had therapy at 10 AM. We were fifteen minutes in when it happened. Grace was working on sentence building. The therapist held up a toy.

"What do you want, Grace?"

Grace stared at it, her face scrunching. "I want... I want..." She couldn't get the words out. Frustration set in.

"It's okay, take your time—"

"I WANT!" Grace grabbed the toy and threw it hard across the room. Then another. And another. "NO! NO! NO!"

Full meltdown. The kind I hadn't seen in weeks. The therapist stayed calm. "Let's take a break—"

But Grace was past breaking. She was screaming, throwing everything she could reach. I tried to hold her. She hit me, kicked, and fought. It took twenty minutes to get her calm enough to leave.

In the car, she cried the whole way home. Not angry crying. Broken crying. I pulled into Linda's driveway and sat there. Grace had been doing so well. Getting better. Healing. Now she was regressing.

Linda came out and saw Grace's red face and my exhausted one.

"Bad session?"

"The worst in months."

Linda helped me get Grace inside. Grace collapsed on the couch, exhausted. "When did she last have a meltdown like that?" Linda asked quietly.

I thought back. "Before I left for New York."

Linda didn't say anything; she didn't need to. The instability had broken something in Grace that my being home wasn't automatically fixing.

That afternoon, while Grace napped, I made a mistake. I googled "FASD regression triggers."

I found article after article about how inconsistent caregiving causes setbacks, how children with FASD need absolute stability, and how even short periods of disruption can undo months of progress. I'd left her for three weeks. I had come back traumatized. I had been physically present but mentally absent. And now she was paying for it.

My phone buzzed. Miranda.

Margaret's attorney just resigned. She's losing support. Ten more days.

Ten more days until what? Until Margaret fell? Until justice happened? Did it really matter if Grace was falling apart? I turned off the phone and put it in the drawer again. It lasted until 8 PM. The pull was too strong. I needed to know what was happening. I turned it back on and read everything I'd missed.

Grace appeared in the doorway, rubbing her eyes. "Mama? You phone again?"

"I'm just checking something, baby."

"You always checking." Her voice was so small. She was right.

Day 7, I promised myself I wouldn't check my phone until Grace was asleep. I made it until lunch. We were eating grilled cheese when it buzzed. I saw Miranda's name. Just one quick look.

Board meeting this morning. Margaret lost three votes. She's vulnerable.

My heart raced. This was it. She was losing. I typed back before I could stop myself: *What happened?*

Grace pushed her plate away. "All done."

"Good job, baby." But I was staring at my phone, waiting for Miranda's response. It came thirty seconds later.

Two board members resigned. One switched to our side. We need 6 votes to remove her. She only has 4 now.

I was reading it when Grace said something.

"What, baby?"

"Go outside?"

"Oh. Yeah. In a minute."

"You always minute." She climbed down, walked away, and didn't ask again.

Day 9, I found the tracker. I'd been checking my phone so obsessively that I discovered you could see historical stock data by the minute. I watched the line graph. Every spike. Every drop. Every trade. Like watching a heartbeat. Margaret's empire dying in real time. I couldn't look away.

Linda found me at 2 AM sitting in the dark, phone glowing, eyes burning. She didn't say anything. She just sat next to me. Finally: "You're not here, are you?"

"I'm right here."

"No. You're in New York. Watching Margaret lose." She paused. "You hid from the fight, but you're still fighting."

The words stung because they were true.

"I don't know how to stop."

"Yes, you do. You just don't want to."

She left me there. I looked at the stock chart: $6.52, up from $6.45 earlier. Miranda's last message: *Everything proceeding as planned. Trust the process.* I turned off the phone. I made it three hours before turning it back on.

Day 11 started with the car. Grace and I were drawing with chalk on the sidewalk in the morning sun. A normal moment.

A black sedan pulled up across the street, parked, and turned off the engine. The driver stayed inside. My chest tightened. Margaret's people. They'd come after me.

"Grace. Inside. Now."

"But Mama—"

"NOW!" My voice came out harsh. Scared. Grace ran. I grabbed her hand too tightly and pulled her toward the house.

"Mama, you're hurting me!"

I loosened my grip but didn't let go. I got her inside and locked the door.

"Mom!"

Linda came running. "What's wrong?"

"Car outside. Someone is following us."

Linda looked through the curtain. "Where?"

"Right there! Black sedan!"

She looked again. "Olivia, I don't—"

The driver got out. Female, in her twenties, holding a package and looking confused at house numbers. She knocked on Mrs. Patterson's door next door. Package delivered. She got back in the car and drove away.

"It was a delivery driver," Linda said quietly.

I couldn't breathe. Couldn't think past the panic. Grace was in the corner, pressed against the wall, eyes huge.

"Mama? You scared?"

"I'm not—" But I was shaking. "I thought someone was—"

"You thought Margaret sent someone." Linda's voice was flat. "You're seeing threats everywhere."

Grace started crying. Not loud, but quietly, the scared kind. I'd terrified my daughter over a delivery driver.

"I'm sorry, baby. Mama made a mistake. Everything's okay." But everything wasn't okay.

That night, after Grace finally fell asleep, Linda sat me down.

"This isn't working."

"What isn't?"

"You hiding. You think you came home, but you didn't. Not really." She gestured at my phone on the table. "You're still in New York. Still at that board meeting. Still fighting Margaret."

"I'm not—"

"You scared Grace today. Hurt her wrist dragging her inside over a delivery driver." Linda's voice cracked. "You can't live like this."

"I'm trying."

"Try harder. Put the phone away. Actually be here."

"What if something happens and I don't know—"

"Then you don't know! Who cares?" Linda stood up. "Grace needs you present. Not checking stock prices. Not reading about Margaret. Here. With her."

She was right. I knew she was right. But I couldn't stop.

Day 12, something in me broke. I woke up at 5 AM and grabbed my phone before I was fully conscious. Stock up to $6.65. News article: "SEC Expands Carrington Investigation." I read it. Then, I read twelve more articles. Then checked Reddit, then Twitter, then forums. I lost track of time.

Grace appeared. "Mama? I'm hungry."

"Okay, I'll make breakfast."

"You said that already."

I looked at the clock. 9:47 AM. I'd been on my phone for four hours. How long had Grace been asking for breakfast?

"I'm sorry, baby. Let me make it now."

I got up, made her cereal, and gave her the bowl. She ate in silence, not looking at me. My phone buzzed. Miranda. I picked it up.

Grace pushed her bowl away, half-eaten, and climbed down.

"Where are you going, baby?"

She didn't answer; she just walked away, stopped in the doorway, and looked back at me.

"You're not my mama anymore."

The words hit like bullets.

"What? Grace, I—"

"You like the phone only." Her voice was matter-of-fact, not angry, just sad. "Linda's my mama now."

She walked away. I sat there, phone in hand, Grace's words echoing. Linda appeared; she had heard everything.

"Put it down."

"Mom, she didn't mean—"

"Put. It. Down."

I put the phone on the table. Linda picked it up and walked to the kitchen. I heard the drawer open and close. She came back and sat across from me.

"You have a choice to make."

"I know, I'm trying to—"

"No. You're not trying. You're pretending to try while staying addicted to watching Margaret fall." Linda's eyes were wet. "Grace just said you're not her mother anymore. Did you hear that?"

I couldn't speak.

"You left her for New York. You came back, but you're still gone. And she's learning to stop needing you because needing you hurts." Linda's voice broke. "So decide. Right now. Are you her mother or are you Margaret's watcher?"

"I want to be her mother."

"Then be her mother. Actually, be it." Linda stood up. "I'm taking Grace to the park. You're staying here. Without your phone. And you're going to figure out what matters more."

She left. I sat alone in the quiet house. Fifteen minutes passed, then thirty, then an hour. The pull to check my phone was physical, like withdrawal, like needing a drink. I understood my father better in that moment than I ever had. This was addiction. Different substance, same disease.

Two hours passed. I thought about Grace's face. "You're not my mama anymore." I reflected on the last two weeks—physically present but mentally in New York. Linda was right. I'd hidden from the fight, but I was still fighting, just from a distance, impotently and obsessively. And Grace was paying the price.

When Linda came home with Grace, I was waiting. Phone still in the drawer. I hadn't touched it.

"Baby, can we talk?"

Grace looked uncertain. "You want to play?"

"I want to say sorry." I knelt down to her level. "You were right. I have been looking at my phone too much."

"You look no more?"

"Not like before. I'm gonna be here. Really here."

She studied my face. "You sure?"

"I'm sure."

She thought about it, then held out her arms. I picked her up, held her, breathed her in.

"I love you, baby."

"Love you too, Mama." She pulled back and looked at me seriously. "Phone again, I am mad."

"Deal."

That night, after Grace was asleep, I took my phone from the drawer. I turned it on one last time. Seventy-two messages from Miranda. Updates about Margaret. Board meetings. SEC investigations. Everything I'd been missing.

I read the last one.

Where are you? Need to discuss next steps. Margaret is vulnerable. Call me.

I typed back.

I can't do this anymore. Keep me updated on major developments only. Otherwise, I'm out.

I sent it, then turned off the phone, put it in the drawer, closed it, and walked away. I made it all night without going back.

On Day 14, Grace woke me up by climbing into my bed and fell back asleep. I lay there holding her. Phone still in the drawer. Dark. Silent.

This was enough. It had to be enough. Because if it wasn 't... if Grace saying "you are not my mama anymore" wasn't enough to break the addiction, then I was more like my father than I'd ever wanted to admit. And that was a thought I couldn't survive.

So I chose this. I chose Grace. I actually chose her this time. Not with words. Not with promises. With action. With silence. By staying present even when every cell in my body wanted to check that drawer.

Tomorrow would be hard. And the day after. And the day after that. But today, right now, Grace was sleeping in my arms. And for once, that was all I needed to know.

Chapter Eleven

Midnight Phone Call

THE PHONE RANG AT midnight. Not my phone. Linda's landline. The one that never rang except for telemarketers and doctor's offices.

I was in Grace's room, watching her sleep like I had every night for twelve days. Making sure her chest rose and fell. Making sure this fragile peace we had built was real. The ringing stopped. Then Linda's voice from downstairs. Muffled. Concerned. Then louder: "Olivia! Phone!"

I moved quickly. Down the stairs. Every muscle tight. Linda was holding the cordless phone, her hand over the mouthpiece. "That woman from New York says it's an emergency."

My stomach dropped. Miranda. I took the phone. "Hello?"

"Thank God." Miranda's voice was wrecked. Raw. Like she had been crying for hours. "Why didn't you answer your phone? I've been calling for six hours. I left twenty-three messages."

My phone. Still in the drawer where I had left it two days ago. "I turned it off."

"For two days?" Her voice cracked. "While everything was—" She couldn't finish. Just made a sound. Half sob, half gasp.

"What happened?"

Silence. Then: "David Keller is dead."

The words hit like a fist. I grabbed the counter. Couldn't breathe. "When?"

"Yesterday. 6:47 PM." Miranda's voice shook. "At his desk. They're saying heart attack. Natural causes."

"They're lying."

"I know." She was crying now. Full breakdown. "But I can't prove it. Heart attack is easy to fake."

Linda was watching me, mouthing: *What's wrong?*

I couldn't answer. Couldn't process. Keller. Dead.

"I tried calling you at seven last night," Miranda continued, her voice breaking. "And eight. And nine. It kept going to voicemail. I thought... I didn't know if you were safe. If Margaret had—"

"You thought she killed me too."

"Yes." Whispered. Broken. "You went completely dark right when Keller died, and I thought—"

"I'm sorry. I was trying to be present and put my phone away. For Grace."

"I know. I understand. But Olivia—" Miranda's voice became firmer. "You can't go dark again. Margaret is moving. This wasn't random. This was strategic."

I looked at Linda. At the stairs leading to Grace's room. "What happens now?"

Miranda took a shaky breath. "Titan Capital is in chaos. Keller was the firm. Without him..." Her voice broke. "The Titan's board is scrambling. The FBI and SEC have opened an investigation into his death, and all active positions are frozen pending review."

"What does that mean for me?"

"You can't sell. Can't vote. Can't do anything for at least sixty days while they investigate." She paused. "But you also can't be margin called. You're frozen. After the investigation, someone will take over as managing partner. Whoever that is will decide what happens to Keller's promises." Miranda's voice was quiet. "I don't know who it'll be yet. The board meets next week."

"So I just... wait?"

"For sixty days, yes. Then we'll know more."

"There's something else," Miranda said. "Keller was working with a whistleblower. Code name Phoenix. Someone inside Carrington Media who documented everything for eight years."

My heart started pounding.

"The gang's money laundering. The RICO violations. Direct connections to Leo's death." Her voice cracked on my brother's name. "Complete evidence. Bank records. Margaret's signatures on everything."

Hope. Sharp and dangerous. "Where's the evidence?"

"That's the problem. Three days before Keller died, Phoenix went dark. The last message said: 'Margaret knows. Going underground. Evidence is hidden. Will contact you later,' and then nothing."

"Keller was killed before Phoenix could tell him where it is."

"Yes." Miranda's voice dropped. "And now Phoenix is hiding. We have no way to find them."

"So why are you calling me?"

"Because Phoenix might contact you. You're the only other person publicly fighting Margaret. You own ten percent of her company. You built the fraud case." She paused. "If Phoenix is going to trust anyone now that Keller's dead, it'll be you."

"That's a stretch."

"Is it? Margaret can't buy you. Can't threaten you into silence."

"She threatened Grace."

"And you're still here. Still alive." Miranda's voice grew urgent. "I need you to come back to New York. Wait for Phoenix to reach out. Help me find them before Margaret does."

"No."

"Olivia—"

"I said no. I chose Grace. I'm staying home."

Linda's face relaxed. Relief. But Miranda wasn't done. "Margaret's been watching you. Surveillance team. Following Grace everywhere."

My blood went cold. "What?"

"I have photos. Grace at preschool. At therapy. At the grocery store with Linda. All from the last week. Margaret's people have been documenting everything."

The room tilted.

"You'll never be free of her," Miranda continued. "Unless we find Phoenix. Get the evidence. Put Margaret in prison."

"You can hide. You can stay home. But you're not safe. Grace isn't. Linda isn't."

I looked at Linda. She'd heard enough. Face white. Scared. "Send me the photos," I said.

"I will. But Olivia, think about it. Margaret killed Keller. She'll kill Phoenix if she finds them first. Then all of this was for nothing."

"I need to go."

"Call me if you change your mind. I need you. I can't do anything alone." Her voice broke again. "And I'm glad you're alive. When you didn't answer, I thought I'd lost you too."

She hung up. I stood there. Phone in my hand. Heart racing. Linda was staring at me. "Keller is dead?"

"Yeah."

"And Margaret's been watching Grace?"

"Yeah."

"Show me the photos."

My phone was still in the drawer. I got it. Turned it on. Eighty-three messages. Forty-seven missed calls.

Miranda's text came through. Six photos attached. I opened them. Grace at preschool. Yesterday. Walking to the playground. Grace at therapy. Tuesday. Coming out of Dr. Reynolds's office. Grace at Morrison's grocery. Monday. Sitting in the cart, pointing at something.

All recent. All since I'd been home. Linda looked over my shoulder. Saw the photos. Made a sound. "They've been following her."

"Yeah."

"While you had your phone off."

The accusation stung because it was true.

"I didn't know."

"Now you do." Linda's voice was flat. "What are you going to do?"

I looked at the photos again. Grace's face. Happy. Oblivious. Safe. Except we now knew that she wasn't safe. None of us were.

"I don't know."

Linda took the phone from me and looked at the photos, her jaw tight. "We can't run from this."

"What?"

"Margaret knows where we are. She's watching. We can't hide." Linda handed back the phone. "So what are we going to do?"

I didn't have an answer.

The next week passed in a fog of paranoia. Every car that drove past felt like a threat. Every person who looked at Grace too long at the playground. Every phone call from an unknown number.

I kept my phone on now, checking it obsessively. Waiting for Phoenix to reach out. Waiting for Margaret's people to make a move. Nothing happened.

Grace went to preschool, had therapy, learned new words, drew pictures, laughed. Normal life. Except I was watching the door every five minutes, checking the windows, making sure the surveillance car wasn't back.

Linda noticed. "You're spiraling again."

"I'm being careful."

"You're being paranoid." But her voice was gentler now. She'd seen the photos too. Knew the threat was real.

By day seven, I'd almost convinced myself Miranda was wrong. Phoenix wasn't going to contact me. Margaret's people were watching but not moving. Maybe we could just exist like this. In limbo. Waiting. Then it was midnight on the seventh day.

Grace was asleep. Linda was asleep. I was in the kitchen, unable to sleep, scrolling through news about Carrington Media for the hundredth time. The stock was at $2.87 now, down from $10 when I'd bought in. I'd lost over seven million dollars. But I was still alive. Then I heard it.

Linda's voice. Sharp. Urgent. "Olivia! Get down here!"

I ran to the front door. Linda was on the porch in her bathrobe, kneeling next to a man collapsed on the steps.

"I heard a noise and came down to check." Her hands were shaking. "He just fell. I think he's been shot."

I looked at him. Thirties. Asian. Expensive suit torn and bloodied. Bullet wound in his side. Blood everywhere.

"Call 911," Linda said.

The man's eyes opened and focused on me. "Olivia Parker?" My stomach dropped. He knew my name.

"Don't," he gasped. "Don't call. They'll find me. Kill me."

"Who will?" Linda asked.

"Margaret's people." He tried to sit up but failed. "I'm Phoenix. The whistleblower. Keller sent me."

My blood went cold. Phoenix. The one with evidence about Leo.

"You need a hospital," Linda said. "You're bleeding out."

"No hospitals. They're watching. They'll kill all of us." His voice was getting weaker. "Please. Just hide me. Two days. Then I'll get the evidence and go."

Linda looked at me. "What's he talking about? Who's Phoenix?"

My mind was racing. Phoenix was here. The man Miranda said might contact me. The one with proof about Margaret. About Leo. "He's the whistleblower from inside Carrington Media. He has evidence about Margaret. About the money laundering. About—" My voice caught. "About Leo."

Linda's face changed. "My son?"

"He has documents. Proof that Margaret paid the gangs that killed him."

Phoenix was watching us, barely conscious. "Leo Parker. April 17, 2014. $240,000 payment authorization. Margaret's signature. I have it. Safe deposit box. Chicago."

The date hit me like a punch. April 17, 2014. The day before Leo died.

"We need to get him inside," I said.

"Olivia—"

"I know. I know what this means. But if he dies, the evidence dies with him."

"And if Margaret finds him here?"

"She's already watching us. She knows where we live." I grabbed Phoenix's arm. "We're already in danger. At least this way, we have a chance."

Linda grabbed his other arm. Between us, we dragged him inside, closed the door, and locked everything. He was heavy. We got him to the couch, blood soaking into Linda's cushions.

"What now?" Linda asked.

Phoenix grabbed my wrist, weak. "No 911. They'll alert Margaret. She has people everywhere."

"Then what? You're going to die if we don't get you help."

"I know someone," I said. "A doctor. Miranda mentioned her. Handles situations like this."

I pulled out my phone and called Miranda. She answered on the second ring. "Olivia? It's midnight. What's—"

"Phoenix is here. At my house. He's been shot. He needs help."

Silence. Then: "Jesus. How bad?"

"Bad. He's losing a lot of blood."

"Don't call 911. I'll get Dr. Rebecca Walsh. She's in Cleveland. Discreet. Handles gunshot wounds, no questions." Miranda was already moving. I could hear her typing on her laptop. "Keep pressure on the wound. Keep him conscious. She'll be there as soon as I reach her."

"How long?"

"I don't know. Let me call her. I'll text you when she's on her way."

"Can you come?"

"I'm in New York. It's a five-hour drive. I'll leave now, but I won't be there until morning." Her voice turned serious. "Olivia, you just made a choice. You understand that?"

"I know."

"Margaret will figure this out. Are you—"

"I know what I did. Just send the doctor."

I hung up. Linda was already working. Towels pressed against the wound. First aid kit open.

"Doctor's coming. I don't know how long."

"Will he make it?"

Phoenix answered. "Have to. Evidence is... too important."

"What's your real name?" I asked.

"Steve Adler. CFO of Carrington Media Group."

Linda's hands stopped moving. "Tyler's CFO?"

"Was. Three years ago, he ordered me to cook the books, inflate subscriber numbers, commit securities fraud." Steve coughed and winced. "I did it. But I kept records. Every email. Every order. Insurance."

"Why come forward now?"

"Because Keller died. Because I knew I was next." His eyes met mine. "Last week, Tyler told Margaret I was the leak. They came for me. I barely got away."

"So you came here."

"Keller said you were the only one who couldn't be bought. Who wouldn't back down. Who had everything to lose if Margaret won." He touched his side, blood seeping through the towels. "He said you'd help."

"He was wrong. I'm hiding. Staying home with my daughter. I'm not fighting anymore."

A sound from upstairs. Grace's door opening. "Mama?"

My heart stopped. Linda moved quickly to the stairs. "It's okay, baby. Gamma's here. Go back to bed."

"What's wrong?"

"Nothing. Just checking on something. Go on now."

Grace's door closed. Linda came back. "She can't see this."

"I know."

"She can't know about any of this."

"I know."

We worked in silence, applying pressure to Steve's wound, keeping him conscious, watching the clock. Twenty minutes. Thirty. Forty. Steve drifted in and out. "Evidence in Chicago... Bank of America... Madison Street... Box 2847..."

"Stay awake," Linda said. "The doctor's coming."

My phone buzzed. A text from Miranda.

Dr. Walsh is on her way. 15 minutes. She's bringing everything she needs.

"Fifteen minutes," I told Linda.

At 12:52 AM, headlights appeared. A car pulled up. A woman got out, carrying two large bags. She moved quickly. I opened the door before she could knock.

"Dr. Walsh?"

"Where is he?"

I led her to Steve. She didn't waste time on questions. She set down her bags and examined him quickly. Professional.

"Bullet went through. That's good. But he's lost a lot of blood. The wound is infected." She looked at me. "He needs a hospital."

"No hospitals," Steve gasped.

"He'll die without proper care."

"He'll die faster if we take him there," I said. "The people who shot him are watching hospitals."

Dr. Walsh was quiet, thinking. Then she opened her bags and started pulling out supplies: IV fluids, antibiotics, surgical equipment. Everything organized and ready.

"Then we do this here. But if complications develop, if the infection spreads, there's nothing I can do."

"Understood."

"I'll need space. Somewhere I can work. This couch won't do."

"Basement," I said. "We can't do this here. Grace might wake up."

Between the three of us, we got Steve downstairs. He could barely stand and nearly passed out twice. Dr. Walsh set up on the old couch, turning our basement into an operating room. She laid out instruments, connected IV lines, and worked with practiced efficiency.

"I need someone to assist," she said.

Linda and I looked at each other. "I will," Linda said.

Dr. Walsh handed her gloves. "Follow my instructions exactly."

They worked for over an hour. I waited upstairs, listening to the sounds below: quiet voices, clinking instruments. Once, Steve made a sound. Not quite a scream, muffled. I stood at the window, watching the empty street, waiting for

Margaret's surveillance car to appear, waiting for everything to break.

My phone was on the table, silent except for one message from Miranda.

On the road. Be there by 6 AM. How is he?

I texted back: *Surgery happening now. Don't know yet.*

The minutes crawled by. I checked on Grace twice. She was still sleeping, her face peaceful and completely unaware.

At 2:34 AM, Dr. Walsh came upstairs, scrubbing blood off her hands in the kitchen sink. "He's stable. Infection under control. But he needs rest. At least ten days before he can travel."

"Ten days?" I said. "He told us two days."

"He was optimistic. That wound needs time to heal. If he moves now, it could rupture. He could die."

Ten days. Steve in our basement. Margaret hunting him. Grace playing upstairs. "Thank you," I said.

Dr. Walsh dried her hands and packed her equipment. "I'll come back tomorrow evening, check the wound, change the bandages." She looked at me. "But after that, you're on your own. And if anyone asks, I was never here."

She left. Linda came upstairs, exhausted, her hands still shaking. "He's asleep, breathing steadily," she said, sitting at the table. "Ten days, Olivia."

"I heard."

"Margaret will figure this out. She has resources, money, people watching this house."

"I know."

"So what do we do?"

"Act normal. Grace goes to preschool, has therapy, lives her life." I looked at the clock: 2:47 AM. "And we pray Margaret's people don't figure it out before Steve heals."

"And if they do?"

I didn't have an answer. Linda went upstairs. "I'm checking on Grace, then trying to sleep. You should too."

But I couldn't sleep. I sat at the kitchen table, staring at the basement door. Steve Adler was down there, with evidence about Leo, about Margaret, about everything. And I'd just hidden him in our house. I knew one thing: Margaret was hunting Steve. And when she figured out he was here, she'd come for all of us.

We had ten days. Ten days to heal, to plan, to get ready for what was coming. Ten days until Margaret found us. Or until we found a way to destroy her first. The clock was ticking, and morning was here, whether we were ready or not.

Chapter Twelve

Hiding a Wanted Man

THE SKY WAS BLEEDING pink. I'd been standing at this window for three hours, watching the street, waiting for Margaret's surveillance car to return, waiting for the moment when everything would end. Steve Adler was in my basement, sleeping, healing, alive. For now.

The clock said 6:11 AM. Last night, a dying man had collapsed on our porch. Linda had found him: Phoenix, the whistleblower with evidence about Leo. And I'd let him in.

Dr. Rebecca Walsh had operated on our basement couch at 1 AM while Grace slept upstairs. Linda had assisted. I'd paced the kitchen, listening to the sounds, the instruments, Steve's muffled scream.

Now he was stable. The infection was controlled, the wound was clean. But he needed ten days before he could travel, ten days before he could get to Chicago, before he could retrieve the evidence that would destroy Margaret.

Headlights appeared. My heart stopped. A car pulled up. Not the surveillance car. A rental. Connecticut plates. Miranda. She got out, looking exhausted, five hours of driving through the night from New York. I opened the door before she could knock.

"How is he?" she asked.

"Stable. Sleeping. Dr. Walsh said ten days before he can travel."

Miranda came inside, saw the bloodstains on the floor that Linda had tried to clean, saw my face, saw the truth. "Show me."

We went to the basement. Steve was on the couch, IV still connected, bandages fresh, breathing steadily. Miranda sat next to him and checked his pulse. "Dr. Walsh is good. He'll make it."

"And then what?"

"Then he goes to Chicago, gets the evidence, and we destroy Margaret." She looked at me. "But Olivia, you understand what you've done. You've hidden a wanted man. Margaret will figure this out."

"How long do we have?"

"I don't know. Days, maybe. A week if we're lucky." Miranda stood. "When she finds out, she won't just come for Steve. She'll come for all of you."

The words settled like lead. We went upstairs. Linda was in the kitchen, making coffee, hadn't slept.

"You made it," Linda said to Miranda.

"Barely. Traffic was hell." Miranda sat at the table. "Tell me everything. Start from when he showed up."

Linda told her: finding Steve on the porch, his bullet wound, Phoenix saying my name, Dr. Walsh arriving with supplies, the surgery in the basement while Grace slept. All of it.

When she finished, Miranda was quiet, thinking. "You did the right thing," she finally said.

"Did we?" Linda's voice was hard. "Because it feels like we just painted a target on this house."

"You already had a target. Margaret's been watching you for weeks. At least now you have leverage."

"Leverage?" I said. "He's a dying man in our basement."

"He's the only person alive who can prove Margaret murdered Keller, who can connect her to Leo's death, who can put her in prison." Miranda pulled out her laptop. "That's not just leverage. That's a nuclear weapon."

"That she'll do anything to destroy."

"Yes. Which is why we need to move fast." Miranda opened a document. "Keller's death triggered SEC and FBI investigations. All his positions are frozen for sixty days while they investigate."

"What does that mean for me?"

"As I said over the phone, you can't sell. Can't vote. Can't do anything." She paused. "But you also can't be margin called. The guarantee is frozen too. You're protected for now."

Relief and dread mixed together.

"What happens after sixty days?"

"That's when things get interesting." Miranda pulled up another file. "Keller's daughter Noreen flew in from London yesterday. She's claiming her inheritance. She wants to take over Titan Capital."

"Keller had a daughter?"

"He never talked about her. They were estranged for fifteen years. But she's his only heir." Miranda's face was serious.

"The problem is, Adam Roth is fighting her. He thinks he should run the fund."

"Who's Adam Roth?"

"Keller's junior partner. Built the fund with him for twenty years. He's competent, ruthless, and he wants your position."

"My position?"

"Your ten percent stake in Carrington Media. Your votes. Your influence." Miranda looked at me. "Noreen wants to honor her father's promises. Keep you protected. Roth wants to use you as a weapon. Make you the public face of the fight."

"No."

"That's what I told him. He said then you're liquidated the moment the SEC freeze ends."

My stomach dropped. "So I have no choice."

"You have a choice. It's just between two people you've never met." Miranda closed her laptop. "The board votes in three days. Whoever wins controls your future."

Linda set down the coffee mugs hard. "This is insane."

"It's reality." Miranda took a cup. "Meanwhile, we have a bigger problem. The FBI investigator who's looking into Keller's death wants to interview Olivia."

"Why me?"

"Because Keller was feeding him information for months. About Margaret. About the fraud. About everything." Miranda looked at me. "His name is Anthony Griffin. He thinks Keller was murdered. And he's right."

"What does he want?"

"You. As a cooperating witness. He wants to build a federal case against Margaret. Criminal charges, not just civil."

"Which means?"

"Which means Margaret doesn't just lose the company. She goes to prison." Miranda paused. "But it also means you'd be working with the FBI. Following their timeline. Their rules. Their protection."

"Or lack of it," Linda said. "We've seen how well the government protects witnesses."

"Better than we can protect ourselves." Miranda looked at both of us. "Right now, you're hiding a wanted man with no backup plan. If Margaret figures out he's here, you're defenseless."

"What are you suggesting?"

"I'm suggesting we need allies. The SEC. The FBI. Noreen Keller. Anyone who can help us survive the next ten days."

Footsteps upstairs. Grace was waking up. "Mama?"

My heart clenched. I went to the stairs. "Morning, baby. Hungry?"

"Yeah. Pancakes?"

"Pancakes."

I went upstairs, got her dressed, and brought her down. I started making breakfast while Grace sat at the table and noticed Miranda. "Who is that?"

"This is Mama's friend Miranda. She came to visit."

"Hi, Grace," Miranda said, smiling, though her eyes were worried. Grace studied her, then looked at me. "Is Mama tired?"

"A little bit, baby."

"Why?"

"Just had trouble sleeping."

"Bad dreams?"

"Yeah. Bad dreams."

Grace finished eating, and Linda took her to the living room to put on cartoons. Miranda and I stayed in the kitchen, speaking quietly.

"She knows something's wrong," Miranda said.

"She always knows."

"Can Linda take her somewhere? A friend's house? Relatives?"

"Linda thinks that would look suspicious. Margaret's people would notice the change."

"So we just keep her here? In the line of fire?"

"What choice do we have?"

Miranda didn't answer because there was no good answer.

I went to check on Steve. He was still sleeping, and his color was better than last night. The IV bag was half empty. He'd live. Dr. Walsh had been clear about that. But living and surviving were different things. Living meant healing for ten days in our basement. Surviving meant Margaret not finding him before then.

I went back upstairs. Miranda was on her laptop, working. "What are you doing?"

"Research. Finding out everything I can about Adam Roth, about Noreen Keller, about who we can trust." She looked up. "Because in three days, one of them takes control of your position. We need to know which one will help us when Margaret comes."

"When. Not if."

"When," Miranda confirmed. "Steve Adler disappeared five days ago. Margaret's been hunting him. She has resources, money, and people. Eventually, someone will talk. Someone will remember seeing him. Someone will trace him here."

"How long?"

"I don't know. Could be tomorrow. Could be next week. But it's coming." Miranda's voice grew more serious. "Which is why we need to be ready. We need to have a plan. We need to know who's on our side when everything breaks."

Linda came back. "Grace wants to go outside and play in the yard."

"No," I said automatically.

"Olivia, she can't stay inside for ten days. She'll know something's wrong."

"Then let her know something's wrong. Better scared than dead."

"She's three years old. She doesn't understand scared versus dead. She just understands Mama won't let her play." Linda's voice was sharp. "And if Margaret's people are watching, seeing Grace cooped up inside will raise more questions than seeing her play normally."

She was right. I knew she was right. "Fine. But stay with her. Don't let her out of your sight."

Linda took Grace to the backyard. I watched from the window. Grace was running, laughing, and picking dandelions. Normal. While a wanted man bled in our basement. While

Margaret hunted him. While Miranda planned our survival. Normal.

"Tell me about Noreen," I said.

Miranda pulled up a file. "Noreen Keller. 34 years old. Yale MBA. Lives in London. Works in private equity. Left the States fifteen years ago after a falling out with her father."

"What kind of falling out?"

"The kind where she told him he cared more about money than family. The kind where he said she was too soft for the business world. They never spoke again."

"Until now."

"Until now. She flew in the day he died. Got a letter from him. Sent before his death." Miranda showed me her phone. A photo of a handwritten letter.

Noreen, if you're reading this, I'm dead. Probably killed by Margaret Carrington. Finish what I started. Take control of Titan Capital. Honor my promises. Especially to Olivia Parker. Find Phoenix. Get the evidence. Destroy Margaret. I love you. Dad.

My throat tightened. "She's fighting Roth because of this letter?"

"She's fighting Roth because her father was murdered. And she wants justice." Miranda put her phone away. "Sound familiar?"

It did. Too familiar. "When is the board vote?"

"Day after tomorrow. 2 PM." Miranda looked at me. "Noreen wants to meet you before then. She wants to understand what her father died protecting."

"I don't want to meet her."

"You don't have a choice. She's flying here tomorrow. To this house. To see Steve. To meet you." Miranda's voice was firm. "Because in three days, she might control your entire position. And she wants to know if you're worth fighting for."

The weight of it pressed down. Noreen Keller. Coming here. To see the man in our basement. To judge whether I deserved her father's protection. While Grace played outside. While Margaret hunted. While the clock ticked down.

"What do I tell her?"

"The truth. About Leo. About Tyler. About everything." Miranda stood. "Because if she's anything like her father, she'll respect honesty more than performance."

My phone buzzed. Text from Dr. Walsh.

Coming by at 6 PM to check on the patient. Any changes?
I texted back: *Stable. Sleeping. No fever.*

Good. See you tonight.

Miranda saw my face. "Dr. Walsh is solid?"

"Linda says yes. She worked with her at the free clinic years ago. Handles gunshot wounds. Doesn't ask questions."

"We'll need her. If Steve's wound gets infected again, if complications develop—"

"I know."

"Do you? Because if Margaret finds him, she'll kill all of you. She won't leave witnesses. Won't take chances. She'll burn this house down with everyone in it."

The words landed like stones. "Then what should I have done? Let him die on the porch?"

"I don't know. Maybe. Maybe that would've been safer." Miranda's voice softened. "But you did what you did. Now we live with it. For ten days. And pray it's enough time."

Grace came running inside. "Mama! Look!" Holding dandelions. Dirty hands. Happy face.

"They're beautiful, baby."

"Make a wish!" She blew. Seeds scattered everywhere.

"What did you wish for?"

Grace thought about it. "More pancakes."

I laughed. It felt like crying. "More pancakes. Good wish."

Linda came in. She saw my face and Miranda's face. "What happened?"

"Nothing. Just planning." I picked up Grace and held her close. "Let's get you cleaned up for lunch."

I took her upstairs, washed her hands, and changed her shirt. The whole time, she chattered about dandelions and wishes.

"Go park tomorrow?"

"Maybe, baby. We'll see."

"Maybe means no."

"Sometimes it means maybe."

She looked at me seriously. "You sad, Mama?"

"A little bit."

"Why?"

"Just grown-up stuff."

"What grown-up stuff?"

"Boring stuff. Nothing for you to worry about."

But she was already worrying. I could see it in her eyes. The same look she'd had after the warehouse, after the nightmares, after every time I'd failed to protect her.

"I love you, baby."

"Love you too, Mama." She hugged me, her small arms tight around my neck.

Grace smiled. "Okay. Lunch now?"

"Lunch now."

We went downstairs. Linda made sandwiches. Grace ate. Miranda worked on her laptop. Steve slept in the basement. Normal. Everything normal. Except nothing was normal. Nothing would ever be normal again.

The clock said 12:47 PM. Day one. Halfway through. Nine and a half days to go. If we survived that long. Miranda stood up. "I need to go back to New York. Work. Keep up appearances. But I'll be back tomorrow with Noreen."

"What time?"

"Afternoon. Maybe 2 PM." She grabbed her bag. "Call me if anything changes. If Steve gets worse. If Margaret's people show up. Anything."

"I will."

She left. Linda and I sat in the quiet, Grace playing with her toys, oblivious.

"Do you regret it?" Linda asked. "Letting him in?"

I thought about it. About Steve's face when he said Leo's name, about Margaret's signature on the payment authorization, about the evidence that could finally prove what happened.

"No."

"Even if it puts Grace at risk?"

"Grace was already at risk. Margaret already knows where we live and has people watching." I looked at my daughter. "At least this way, we have a chance to end it."

Linda stood up. "Then we better make these ten days count."

She went to the basement, checked on Steve, changed his bandages, and made sure the IV was flowing.

I stayed with Grace, played blocks, read books, pretended everything was fine. But I kept looking at the window, at the empty street, at the space where Margaret's surveillance car usually parked. It wasn't there. It hadn't been there for a while. That should have been comforting. Instead, it felt like waiting, like Margaret was planning something, like the calm before the storm.

At 6 PM, Dr. Walsh arrived, checked Steve's wound, changed the dressing, and gave him more antibiotics. "He's healing well. Better than expected." She packed her bag. "Keep him hydrated. Keep the wound clean. I'll check again tomorrow."

She left. Night fell. I put Grace to bed, read her three stories, and stayed until she fell asleep. The clock read 11:23 PM. Day one was almost over.

Nine days to go. I sat in the darkness, listening to the house settle, listening to Grace breathe upstairs, and listening to Steve shift on the couch below.

The street outside was empty, dark, and quiet. But I knew it wouldn't last. Margaret was coming. And when she did, we'd all be here. Together. Trapped. The choice I'd made when I let Steve in would finally come due, whether we were ready or not.

Chapter Thirteen

They're Here

THE SCREAM CAME FROM the basement. Not loud. Muffled. But unmistakable. Steve.

Grace's spoon stopped halfway to her mouth. Cheerios dripped milk back into the bowl. Little drops hit the table. Tiny splashes. "What's that?"

My chest tightened. Like someone pressing down hard. I couldn't breathe right. "Nothing, baby. Just the TV."

I stood. My legs felt heavy. Wrong. But I made them move slowly. Normal speed. Like mothers do when everything's fine. "Eat your breakfast."

Grace went back to her cereal, humming some song from her cartoons. The sound was so light. So normal. It hurt to hear it.

Linda was already at the basement door. Her face told me everything before she said a word. Eyes too wide. Mouth tight. The look nurses get right before they run.

We went down together. Each step creaked under our weight. The basement smelled wrong. Sweat and copper and something sour underneath. The kind of smell that means bodies breaking down.

Steve was on the couch, shaking so hard the whole thing rattled. Fever sweat had soaked through his shirt and into the cushions beneath him. Dark patches spread. The bandage on his side wasn't white anymore. It was red. Not pink spotted. Not rust-colored at the edges. Completely red. Blood seeped through the gauze. Through the tape. Pooling.

"It's infected again." Linda's voice came out too calm. Flat. The nurse voice. The one that means she's screaming inside. "Worse than before."

Steve's eyes opened. They looked past me. Through me. Pupils blown wide and black. "Chicago. Need to... get to Chicago..."

I touched his forehead. My hand jerked back on its own. Like touching a stove burner. Way too hot. Burning. "You're not going anywhere." My voice sounded steadier than the shaking in my hands. "Mom, call Dr. Walsh."

"She's not coming until tonight."

"Tell her it's urgent. Tell her—" I swallowed. Tell her he might be dying. Tell her we might lose him before he can testify. "Tell her he's getting worse."

Linda ran upstairs. I heard her voice filtering down. Urgent but quiet. Trying not to scare Grace.

I stayed with Steve. My hands shook as I peeled back the bandage. Slow. Careful. But I already knew what I'd find. The wound looked angry. That's the only word for it. Swollen and red. The edges hot to touch. Red lines spread out from the center like cracks in glass. Like poison in water.

Dr. Walsh had warned this could happen. Warned that infection could turn bad fast in gunshot wounds. Warned that waiting too long meant sepsis. Meant death.

"How long?" Steve's voice was barely there. Cracked and dry. Like old paper.

"Until you can travel? At least a week. Maybe more now."

"Don't have a week." His hand shot out, grabbing my wrist. The grip was weak but desperate. Fingers too hot against my skin. "Margaret... she's close. Can feel it."

"You're delirious. The fever—"

"No." His eyes found mine. Suddenly clear. Too clear. Like the moment before a storm breaks. "I know her. I know how she thinks. Twelve years working for that woman. I know."

A cough. When he pulled his hand away, there was blood on his lips. Just a little. Just enough. "She's figured it out. Where I went. Who helped me." His breathing came fast and shallow. "She's just waiting for the right moment."

Footsteps above us. Grace running from room to room. Playing. Humming to herself. Safe. Protected. For now. "Then we move you," I said. "Somewhere else. Somewhere safer."

"Nowhere is safer." He closed his eyes. "She owns this town. Has people everywhere. Police. Judges. Some FBI agents."

His grip on my wrist tightened again. It hurt this time. "Just need to hold on. Get to Chicago. Get the evidence. Then it's over."

Linda came down the stairs. "Dr. Walsh will be here in an hour. She's bringing stronger antibiotics."

"Good."

But Steve had already passed out again. His hand fell away from my wrist, leaving a hot print on my skin. His breathing sounded wrong. Too fast and too shallow at the same time. Like drowning on dry land.

We went back upstairs. Closed the basement door softly enough that Grace wouldn't notice. She was done with breakfast. Bowl in the sink. Hands sticky with milk. She looked up at me with Leo's eyes. Dark and trusting. "Can I watch cartoons?"

"Yeah, baby."

I turned on the TV. Sat with her on the couch. Pulled her close. She smelled like cereal and strawberry shampoo. Like normal mornings. Like the life we used to have before guns and blood and men dying in basements. She leaned against me. Warm. Real. Everything I had left to protect. But all I could think about was Steve's words.

She's close. I can feel it.

And the blood. So much blood soaking through that bandage. The red spreading like it had a mind of its own. I held Grace tighter. Watched cartoon characters chase each other across the screen. Their bright colors and simple problems. Cat chases mouse. Mouse escapes. Everyone laughs. Simple. Safe. Nothing like the world we were living in now.

I listened for sounds from the basement. For Steve crying out. For the infection winning. For everything ending before we could finish what Leo started. Grace fell asleep against me. Her breath soft and even. Trusting me to keep her safe. I didn't know if I could anymore.

The house settled around us. Old pipes creaking. Furnace kicking on. Normal sounds that felt all wrong now. Every noise made me jump. Every car passing outside made my heart race. Waiting for the knock. For Margaret's people to figure out where Steve was hiding.

Dr. Walsh arrived at 10:15 AM. I met her at the door. Quiet. Fast. Didn't want Grace waking up. "Where is he?"

"Basement."

We went down together. Dr. Walsh didn't waste time. She checked Steve's vitals: his temperature, his pulse, and the wound. Her face tightened with each thing she examined, small lines appearing around her mouth. The professional mask was cracking.

"One-oh-three point seven." She set down the thermometer and wiped it with an alcohol pad. "Blood pressure's dropping. Pulse is one-twenty. Rapid and weak. This isn't good, Olivia."

She changed the bandage. I watched her face change too, noticed the professional mask slipping just a little. I saw fear underneath.

"I need to debride this. Clean out the infected tissue." She pulled supplies from her bag. "It's going to hurt."

"He's barely conscious."

"I know. That's the only mercy here."

She worked fast and precise, but not gently. She couldn't be gentle. Steve screamed twice, deep animal sounds that didn't sound human. It woke Grace upstairs. I heard her calling for me, but Linda got to her first. She kept her away, kept her safe from seeing this.

The smell worsened as Dr. Walsh worked, sweet and rotten. I had to breathe through my mouth and turn my head. But I made myself watch, made myself see what hiding Steve was costing.

Twenty minutes. That's how long it took. Dr. Walsh's hands were steady the whole time, even though mine were shaking just from watching. When she finished, there was blood on her gloves, under her fingernails, smeared on her wrist where the glove didn't quite reach.

She washed her hands in the utility sink, using the harsh orange soap that smelled like chemicals. She scrubbed hard and didn't look at me for a long time.

"He needs a hospital. Proper imaging, IV antibiotics around the clock, possibly surgery." She dried her hands but still wouldn't meet my eyes. "This is beyond what I can do here."

"You know we can't do that."

"I know. But I'm telling you anyway." She finally looked at me. "The antibiotics will help. But if this gets worse, if the infection spreads to his bloodstream..." She didn't finish. She didn't need to.

"How long does he have?"

"I don't know. Days. Maybe a week if we're lucky and the antibiotics work." She packed up her supplies, her movements sharp and angry. "But I can't promise anything. Bodies are unpredictable, especially those that have been shot and are hiding in basements instead of getting proper care."

She left. I stayed in the basement. I watched Steve sleep, observed his chest rise and fall, counting breaths, making sure each one came. His face was gray, sweat beading on his forehead.

The new bandage was white and clean, but I knew what was underneath. I knew it was eating him alive from the inside. I knew we were running out of time.

Upstairs, Grace was crying. "Want Mama!"

"I'm coming, baby."

I went up and held her. She wrapped her arms around my neck and squeezed tight as if afraid I'd disappear. "You okay?"

"Yeah. I'm okay."

"Who's screaming?"

"TV. Just the TV, baby." The lie tasted bitter. "Bad guy in the movie."

She looked at me with those dark eyes. Leo's eyes. Like she knew I was lying but loved me too much to say it. Or maybe she was just three. Innocent enough to believe me.

"I'm hungry."

"Okay. Let's make lunch."

I made grilled cheese, her favorite. Cut it into triangles the way she liked. No crusts. Poured juice into her special cup with the elephants on it. Watched her eat. Every bite normal and perfect, everything I needed to protect.

Linda came into the kitchen. Poured coffee. The smell made my stomach turn. I hadn't eaten since yesterday and couldn't remember when I'd slept more than an hour. She didn't say anything for a long time. Just stood at the window, looking out. Watching. Then: "Walsh is right. This is too dangerous."

"I know."

"We should call the FBI. Tell them everything. Get protection."

"Steve says they have leaks. That Margaret has people inside."

"Maybe. But maybe that's paranoia talking." Linda sipped her coffee, grimacing like it was too hot. "Or maybe we're all going to die because we trusted the wrong person."

I didn't answer. Didn't have an answer. Grace finished her sandwich, juice running down her chin. I wiped it away with a napkin. Gently. "Go play, baby."

She ran off, happy. Safe. Oblivious to the fact that everything was falling apart around her. Linda and I stayed in the kitchen. The silence was heavy between us, weighted with all the things we weren't saying.

She went back to the basement to check on Steve, to change the IV bag, to do what nurses do when people are dying and there's nothing else to do but wait.

I stayed in the kitchen, watching Grace play with her dolls in the living room, making them talk to each other. Simple stories. Happy endings. The way the world should work but never does. I listened for sounds that didn't belong. For cars pulling up. For doors opening. But the street stayed quiet.

Normal. Neighbors walking dogs. Kids riding bikes. The whole world pretending everything was fine.

The doorbell rang at 11:47 AM. Too early for Dr. Walsh's evening check-in. My stomach dropped. My heart hammered against my ribs. I went to the door slowly, each step deliberate. I looked through the peephole. A woman in her thirties, wearing a business suit. Expensive. Navy blue with sharp lines. Standing next to Miranda. I didn't recognize her. I scanned her hands. No weapon visible. Scanned behind them. No cars that didn't belong. No men in suits waiting.

My hand went to my phone anyway, ready to call 911. Ready to grab Grace and run. Miranda saw me through the glass. Must have seen my shadow. She shook her head slightly, mouthed something I couldn't make out. Then clearer: "It's okay."

I opened the door, chain still on. Cold air rushed in. "Who is this?"

"Olivia. This is Noreen Keller." Miranda's voice was calm. Professional. But I could see tension around her eyes and in the way she held her shoulders. "We need to talk."

Noreen Keller. The woman whose father died because of all this. The woman who had been estranged from her father for fifteen years and only spoke at his funeral. I studied her through the gap, looking for tells, for signs this was a trap. She looked back at me, direct. No warmth, but no hostility either. Just tired, like she had been up all night. I unlatched the chain, let them in, and locked it behind them quickly.

"Grace, go play in your room for a bit."

"But Mama—"

"Room. Now." That tone. The one that meant non-negotiable. The one I hated using but needed sometimes.

Grace heard it and saw something in my face that made her stop arguing. She went upstairs, dragging her feet but complying. I watched her until she disappeared. We sat at the kitchen table. Linda brought coffee nobody wanted. The cups just sat there, getting cold, leaving rings on the wood.

Noreen looked at me, direct. No warmth. "Miranda told me about Steve Adler. I need to see him."

"He's sick. High fever. Infection. Dr. Walsh just left."

"I understand. I still need to see him."

Something in her voice. Hard. Certain. This wasn't a request. This was someone used to getting what they wanted. Someone used to power. I looked at her hands, watched how she held herself, searching for weapons, for wires, for anything that indicated this was a setup. But she just looked tired, determined, angry underneath.

I glanced at Miranda. She nodded once, a small movement, her way of saying it was okay, that Noreen could be trusted. But Miranda had worked for Keller, and Keller was dead. So maybe trust wasn't the right word anymore.

"Okay."

We went down to the basement. The stairs creaked, every sound too loud, every footstep announcing us. Steve was awake, barely. He saw us coming. His eyes focused on Noreen. Recognition clicked. Something changed in his face. Fear, maybe. Or shame.

"Keller's daughter."

"I am." She sat on the edge of the couch, not too close, keeping distance between them. She studied him, his face, the fever sweat, the IV line snaking into his arm, the bandage showing pink. "You worked for Margaret Carrington for twelve years."

"Yes."

"Cooked the books, committed fraud, helped her launder money, helped her kill people."

"Yes."

"Why should I trust you?"

Steve was quiet for a moment, breathing hard, his chest rising and falling too quickly. Then: "You shouldn't. I'm guilty. Everything I did, I did willingly." He coughed, winced, pain flashing across his face. "For money. For career advancement. For all the wrong reasons."

"Then why come forward now? Why not stay hidden? Take your chances?"

"Because your father was murdered." The words came out flat. Honest. No emotion in them. Like he'd said them so many times that they didn't mean anything anymore.

"Because Margaret killed him. Because I'm tired of being scared." He looked at her. Really looked at her.

Noreen's face stayed blank. Professional. But I saw her jaw tighten. I saw her hands clench on her knees. White knuckles showing. "Tell me about the evidence."

Steve told her everything. Eight years of documentation. Wire transfers. Shell companies. Offshore accounts. Bank statements showing $2.4 million going to the Scorpions gang. Margaret's signatures on authorization forms. Her handwriting on memos. Emails explicitly discussing how to hide the payments. The connection to seven deaths. Including Leo Parker. Including her father. Safe deposit box in Chicago. Key hidden in his apartment. Everything documented. Everything traceable. Enough to put Margaret away for life.

His voice got weaker as he talked. Fading in and out. But he kept going. Pushing through the fever. Through the pain. Getting it all out. When he finished, Noreen stood. Paced to the window. Back again. Her heels sharp on the concrete floor. Click. Click. Click. Like a countdown.

"How do I know you're telling the truth? How do I know this isn't Margaret sending someone to flush out what we know?"

Steve reached under his pillow. Moved slowly. Carefully. Every movement costing him. Pulled out a thumb drive. "Samples. Enough to prove what's in Chicago is real."

He held it out to her. Noreen stared at it. Didn't take it. "What's on there?"

"Bank statements. Emails. Transaction records. Photos of documents." Steve's hand shook. The thumb drive trembling. "Everything you need to understand what Margaret did. How she did it. Who helped her."

"And you're on there too? Your involvement?"

"Yes. I'm not pretending I'm innocent. I'm guilty. I'll go to prison." He kept his hand extended. "But so will Margaret. That's worth it."

Noreen took the thumb drive. Held it like it might explode. Turned it over in her hands. "This is real?"

"It's real."

She looked at Miranda. "We need a laptop. Somewhere we can look at this without being seen."

"My rental car. Tinted windows. Give me two minutes."

Miranda went upstairs. We waited. The silence was heavy. Noreen kept turning the thumb drive over, looking at it like she could see through the plastic to the data inside. Noreen walked back to the window. Looked out at the small slice of yard visible from down here. Dead grass. Bare trees. Gray sky. "My father died helping you. Did you know that?"

"I knew he was asking questions. I knew Margaret was worried about it. Worried enough to do something," Steve said.

"And you didn't warn him."

"No."

"Why not?"

"Because I was a coward. Because I was trying to save myself." Steve's voice grew quieter, harder to hear. "Because I hoped if I stayed quiet, if I kept my head down, maybe she'd leave me alone. Maybe I could ride it out. Wait for someone else to take her down."

"Did she leave you alone?"

"No. She sent someone to kill me. Almost succeeded." He gestured weakly at his wound. "That's when I realized you can't hide from Margaret. You can't wait her out. She always wins unless someone stops her."

"So you're stopping her now? Out of guilt? Conscience?"

"Out of survival. Out of knowing I'm dead either way." He closed his eyes. "Might as well take her with me."

Noreen didn't respond to that. She just kept looking out the window. Miranda came back, a laptop under her arm. "My car has tinted windows. No one can see in. We should be safe."

"Good. Let's go."

They headed for the stairs. Noreen stopped and looked back at Steve. "If this is fake, if you're playing us, if this is some scheme to protect Margaret—" She didn't finish the threat; she didn't need to. Her voice said it all.

"It's not fake."

She went upstairs. Miranda followed. I listened to their footsteps, the front door opening and closing. I stayed with Steve. The silence felt better than talking, better than thinking about what came next.

"You okay?" I asked.

He opened his eyes. "That's a stupid question."

"Yeah. Sorry."

"She hates me."

"Can you blame her?"

"No." He closed his eyes again. "Her father was a good man. Better than me. Better than most people I know."

"Then why did you help Margaret kill him?"

"I didn't help her kill him. I just didn't stop it. I failed to warn him." His breathing became ragged. "There's a difference. Not a big one, but it matters to me."

I didn't know what to say to that. I didn't know if the difference mattered. Dead was dead either way.

I watched from the living room window. Miranda's rental car sat in the driveway. A dark sedan with tinted windows, just like she said. I could see shapes moving inside, shadows shifting, nothing clear. Linda came up behind me. "What are they doing?"

"Looking at the evidence. Deciding if Steve's telling the truth."

"And if they decide he's not?"

"Then we're alone in this." I stepped back from the window but couldn't stop watching the car, couldn't stop thinking about what they were seeing. "Just us and a dying man in our basement."

Grace came downstairs. "Mama, I'm bored."

"Want to color?"

"Yeah!"

I set her up at the kitchen table with crayons and paper. She drew circles and called them flowers. Drew stick figures and called them family. Me, her, and Linda. I sat with her and pretended everything was normal, pretended there weren't people in our driveway looking at evidence that could get us all killed.

Twenty-three minutes. That's how long they stayed in the car. When they came back inside, Noreen's face had changed. Pale. Tight. Her hands shook slightly when she set the laptop down on the counter. The confident businesswoman was gone. Just someone who'd seen something they couldn't unsee.

"It's real." Her voice came out rough, like she'd been crying or screaming. "All of it. Everything he said. More, actually."

"You didn't believe him?"

"I wanted to. But evidence and belief are different things." She sat down heavily, as if her legs had stopped working. "My father died because of this. Because he was helping Steve. Trying to expose Margaret. Trying to do the right thing."

"I'm sorry."

"Don't be sorry." She looked up at me, her eyes red and raw. "Help me finish what he started. Help me destroy her."

Miranda pulled out her phone and checked something. Her face went tight, that professional mask cracking.

"What?" I asked.

"The board vote is tomorrow morning at nine AM. Adam Roth versus Noreen for control of Titan Capital." She looked at Noreen. "The winner controls everything: the company, Olivia's position, your father's legacy."

Noreen nodded. "Roth wants to liquidate. Sell all positions, including yours." She looked at me. "Walk away with whatever money is left and forget any of this happened. Cut losses. Move on."

My stomach dropped. "Why?"

"Because fighting Margaret is expensive. Dangerous. Bad for business." Noreen's voice turned hard and bitter. "He thinks my father died because he was reckless. That activism doesn't pay. That we should have sold out years ago."

"And you?"

"I think Margaret Carrington murdered my father. Had him killed because he was getting close. Because he wouldn't stop." She leaned forward. "And I'm going to destroy her. But I need to know something first. Are you in this fight? Really in it? Or are you just hiding?"

The question sat between us, heavy and demanding an answer I didn't have. Linda stood in the doorway, watching and judging. Grace was at the table, coloring, safe for this moment. Steve was in the basement, dying, maybe.

"I don't know," I said, honest and raw, too tired to lie. "I want Margaret destroyed. I want justice for Leo, for your father, for everyone she's hurt. But I also have a three-year-old daughter who needs her mother alive."

"So does everyone." Noreen stood and paced to the window. "So does every person Margaret has hurt. Every family she's destroyed. Every child who lost a parent because of her greed. But if everyone hides, she wins. She keeps winning. Forever."

"That's easy to say when it's not your daughter at risk."

"My father is dead." Noreen's voice cracked just a little, enough to show real emotion beneath the hardness. "You think that's not a risk I understand? You think I don't know what it costs?"

"Your father chose to fight. Grace doesn't get to choose. She's three."

"No. She gets to live in whatever world we leave her." Noreen walked back to the window and looked out at the street. Normal. Quiet. "You want her growing up knowing people like Margaret can kill without consequences? That money and power mean you're untouchable? That good people die while monsters prosper?"

I didn't answer. I didn't know how to. Because she was right. And she was wrong. And Grace was three, and none of this should be her burden.

Miranda's phone rang, loud in the quiet kitchen. She glanced at the screen. "My contact at the FBI."

"FBI?" My voice came out sharp. "You've been talking to the FBI?"

"I've been feeding them information for months. About Margaret. About Carrington Media. Everything we could find," she replied. "This is Miranda. Yes. When? How many?"

Her expression changed. Her eyes widened, color draining. "You're sure? Both of them?"

She hung up and looked at us. I knew before she said it that everything had just changed.

"FBI raided Carrington Media headquarters two hours ago. Federal agents. Search warrants. They went through everything. Servers, files, personal offices."

The room went silent. Even Grace stopped coloring.

"Margaret was arrested. Tyler was arrested. Both of them." Miranda's voice shook slightly. "Both released on bail within ninety minutes."

My breath stopped. "What does that mean?"

"It means the government is moving. Building a case. They have enough for a raid. For arrests. But not enough to hold them yet." Miranda pulled up a news site on her phone and showed me. "It means Margaret knows we're coming. Knows the FBI is investigating. And she's going to start cleaning up loose ends."

FBI RAIDS CARRINGTON MEDIA IN FRAUD INVESTIGATION

Video footage showed FBI agents in windbreakers carrying boxes out of the Carrington building. Margaret in handcuffs, being led to a car. Her face was stone. No emotion. Tyler was behind her, wearing the same expression, as if getting arrested was just another inconvenience. Stock price ticker at the bottom: CMG 31% down from $6.50 to $4.50.

"It's crashing," Miranda said. "Investors are panicking. Running."

"Good." Noreen's voice was cold, hard as iron. "Let it crash. Let her lose everything."

"But Olivia loses too. Her position—"

"Is frozen by SEC order pending the investigation. She can't sell anyway." Noreen looked at me. "You're locked in for a minimum of sixty days. Which means you're committed whether you like it or not. Whether you're ready or not."

The words hit me like cold water. Like drowning. Committed. Locked in. No escape. No running.

The basement door opened. Linda. "Steve's asking for you. Both of you."

We went down. Steve was sitting up. Barely. He saw the news on Miranda's phone—the video of Margaret getting arrested—and smiled. Weak. Sick. But real.

"She knows," he said. "She knows they're coming. She'll move fast now. Clean up. Destroy evidence. Kill witnesses."

"We have copies—" Noreen started.

"Doesn't matter. She'll make the originals disappear. Make it look like fraud. Like I made it all up." He coughed, harder this time. Blood on his lips. "Need to get to Chicago. Now. Before she does."

"You can't travel. The infection—"

"I die here or I die trying. Either way." He looked at Noreen. "Your father understood that. Understood some things are worth dying for. Do you?"

Noreen stared at him, and for the first time, I saw uncertainty in her face. I saw fear. "The board votes tomorrow," she said quietly. "If I lose, Roth liquidates everything. We lose our position. Our leverage. Everything my father built."

"Then don't lose."

"It's not that simple."

"It never is." Steve lay back down. "But you have the evidence now. Show them. Show them what Margaret did. Show them your father died trying to stop her. Make them choose a side."

We went back upstairs. Noreen pulled Miranda aside. Quiet. Urgent.

"I need you in New York. Tonight. The board's going to panic after this FBI raid. Roth will use it against me, saying Margaret's arrest proves my father was reckless. That activism is too dangerous."

Noreen glanced at the basement door. "I'm staying here. I need to get more from Steve. Details about the evidence. Names. Dates. Everything that'll convince the board this isn't just revenge. But you need to be there. Talk to the members I trust. Remind them why my father fought. Remind them what we're fighting for."

Miranda nodded, already pulling out her phone. Checking flights. "I can be there by midnight. Start making calls first thing." She looked at me, at Linda, at the basement. "You'll be okay here?"

"We'll manage," I said. "Go. Do what you need to do."

Miranda grabbed her bag and keys. Headed for the door, then stopped and turned back to Noreen. "Your father would be proud of you. Fighting like this. Not giving up."

Then she was gone. Engine starting. Taillights disappearing down the street. And we were one person fewer. One ally gone. The walls closing in.

Grace needed dinner. Life kept moving even when everything was falling apart. I made pasta. Butter and salt. Grace ate it happily, oblivious to the fact that federal agents had raided Margaret's headquarters. That our position was frozen. That

Steve might be dying. That everything was accelerating toward some ending I couldn't see yet.

After dinner, Linda and I sat at the table. Noreen was on her phone, calling board members. Making her case. Her voice low but intense, fighting for control of her father's company.

"We're trapped," Linda said quietly. "The FBI knows about Steve. Margaret knows about Steve. It's only a matter of time."

"I know."

"We should leave. Tonight. Pack up Grace and go."

"Where?"

"Anywhere Margaret isn't."

"That's nowhere."

"Steve. Shot. Infected. Hiding in our basement. Waiting to see if he dies from infection or from Margaret's people." She looked at me. "We're next. You know that, right? Once Margaret decides we're a threat, we're next."

"Maybe."

"Not maybe. Definitely." Linda stood and started clearing dishes. "I love you, Olivia. You're family. But I need you to think about Grace. Really think about her. Not about justice. Not about Leo. Just about keeping that little girl alive."

Linda went upstairs. I stayed at the table, watching Grace play, listening to Noreen fight for control, and thinking about Linda's words. We're next.

At 6:47 PM, I looked out the window. The surveillance car was back. A black sedan. The same one that had been watching us for weeks. Parked across the street. Engine off. The driver visible. Watching. My chest went tight. I couldn't breathe properly.

Linda saw my face and came to the window. "How long?"

"Just saw it. Could have been there for hours."

"Call Noreen."

I did. Noreen came to the window and looked at the car. Her face didn't change. Professional mask back in place. "Same one?"

"I think so."

"Have they done anything? Gotten out? Made calls?"

"Not yet."

Noreen pulled out her phone. Took photos. License plate. Driver. Car model. "I'll run this. See if it's registered to Margaret or one of her shell companies."

The driver's door opened. We all froze. A man got out. Thirties. Suit. Not casual surveillance clothes. Professional.

He looked at our house. Direct. No pretense of hiding. Then pulled out his phone and made a call.

"He's calling someone," Linda whispered.

The man talked for maybe thirty seconds. Nodded. Hung up. Didn't get back in the car. Just stood there. Waiting. Watching us watch him.

"What does that mean?" I asked.

"It means Margaret knows Steve is here." Noreen's voice was flat. Empty. "And she's deciding what to do about it."

"We need to call the FBI—"

"No. Steve's right. They have leaks. Margaret will know within an hour." Noreen kept watching the man. "We need to get Steve out of here. Tonight. Before they come."

"He can't travel. Dr. Walsh said—"

"I don't care what Dr. Walsh said. That man outside? He's not surveillance. He's advance. Margaret's sending a team. Maybe tonight. Maybe tomorrow. But soon."

My phone rang. Unknown number. My heart stopped.

"Don't answer it," Noreen said.

But I already was. Couldn't help it. "Hello?"

"Ms. Parker. This is FBI Agent Anthony Griffin. I need to speak with you about Steve Adler."

My blood went cold. "How did you—"

"We've been tracking him since he disappeared five days ago. We know he came to Cleveland. We know he's at your house." Griffin's voice was calm. Professional. Almost bored. "I need you to listen carefully. You're in danger. Margaret Carrington has people watching your house right now. I've been monitoring the situation. I'm coming to bring you and Steve Adler into protective custody."

"How do I know you're FBI? How do I know you're not working for Margaret?"

"Because if I were working for her, you'd already be dead." A pause. "I'll be at your house in twenty minutes. Don't open the door for anyone else. Don't let anyone in. Don't let anyone out. Do you understand?"

"I—"

"Twenty minutes, Ms. Parker. Be ready."

He hung up. I looked at Noreen. At Linda. At Grace, playing with her dolls. "FBI Agent Anthony Griffin. He says he knows Steve is here. Says he's coming to help us."

Noreen's face didn't change. "And you believe him?"

"I don't know."

"Neither do I." She looked out at the surveillance car. The man was still standing there. Still watching. "But right now, we don't have a choice. Margaret knows where we are. The FBI knows where we are. We're trapped."

The man across the street got back in his car, started the engine, but didn't leave. Just sat there. Waiting. Grace came over to me. "Mama, I'm tired."

"Okay, baby. Let's get you ready for bed."

But I didn't move. Couldn't move. Just stood there watching the surveillance car. Watching our house become a cage. Watching everything close in.

Twenty minutes. That's all we had. Twenty minutes until the FBI showed up. Or until Margaret's people did. Or until everything finally broke.

I picked up Grace and held her close. She smelled like pasta and soap. Normal things. Safe things.

"It's okay, baby," I whispered. "Everything's going to be okay." But I didn't believe it. And I don't think she did either.

Outside, the surveillance car waited. Inside, we did the same. Waiting for the knock at the door that would change everything.

Chapter Fourteen

Author's Note

THANK YOU VERY MUCH for spending time with **Book 4, *Where Leo Died*,** in the five-book saga The Daughter of a Drunk.

Olivia just learned what it costs to threaten the Carrington empire. Margaret knows exactly how to break her. And Grace is paying the price.

Book 5: His Name Everywhere is live now. This is where everything Olivia has built either holds or shatters completely. The final book. The final choice.

Don't wait to find out what happens next.

Just search "His Name Everywhere by Howard Kane" wherever you buy books.

A quick favor: If this story has meant something to you, if Olivia's impossible choices, the weight of everything at stake, or a mother's desperate fight resonated, would you leave a short review wherever you purchased the book? Even 2-3 sentences help other readers find these books. It makes a real difference.

Thank you for reading.

With gratitude,

Howard Kane

278

This page was intentionally left blank.

This page was intentionally left blank.

This page was intentionally left blank.

This page was intentionally left blank.

www.ingramcontent.com/pod-product-compliance
Lightning Source LLC
Chambersburg PA
CBHW020133310726
48970CB00006B/1849